"I have a confession to make, Sam Zachary,"

Laura said as she traced the rim of her glass with a fingertip. "I thought I had made a big mistake about hiring you. I was even thinking, earlier tonight, about asking you for a refund, and hiring somebody different."

Sam raised an eyebrow. "And?"

"I know now I didn't make a mistake. I feel safe with you."

She wouldn't have, Sam thought, if she knew the direction in which his mind was tending while his gaze roamed unhindered over her relaxed face and figure. About all that separated him from the thugs he had just taken care of was a willingness to obey the law. That and the fact that they were in a public place. Otherwise...

Otherwise, what, for God's sake?

Dear Reader,

As the Intimate Moments quarter of our yearlong 20th anniversary promotion draws to a close, we offer you a month so full of reading excitement, you'll hardly know where to start. How about with *Night Shield*, the newest NIGHT TALES title from *New York Times* bestselling author Nora Roberts? As always, Nora delivers characters you'll never forget and a plot guaranteed to keep you turning the pages. And don't miss our special NIGHT TALES reissue, also available this month wherever you buy books.

What next? How about *Night of No Return*, rising star Eileen Wilks's contribution to our in-line continuity, A YEAR OF LOVING DANGEROUSLY? This emotional and suspenseful tale will have you on the edge of your seat—and longing for the next book in the series. As an additional treat this month, we offer you an in-line continuation of our extremely popular out-of-series continuity, 36 HOURS. Bestselling author Susan Mallery kicks things off with *Cinderella for a Night.* You'll love this book, along with the three Intimate Moments novels— and one stand-alone Christmas anthology—that follow it.

Rounding out the month, we have a new book from Beverly Bird, one of the authors who helped define Intimate Moments in its very first month of publication. She's joined by Mary McBride and Virginia Kantra, each of whom contributes a top-notch novel to the month.

Next month, look for a special two-in-one volume by Maggie Shayne and Marilyn Pappano, called *Who Do You Love?* And in November, watch for the debut of our stunning new cover design.

Leslie J. Wainger
Executive Senior Editor

Please address questions and book requests to:
Silhouette Reader Service
U.S.: 3010 Walden Ave., P.O. Box 1325, Buffalo, NY 14269
Canadian: P.O. Box 609, Fort Erie, Ont. L2A 5X3

BLUER THAN VELVET
MARY McBRIDE

Published by Silhouette Books
America's Publisher of Contemporary Romance

For my editor
Margaret O'Neill Marbury,
with gratitude and much affection

 SILHOUETTE BOOKS

ISBN 0-373-27101-8

BLUER THAN VELVET

Copyright © 2000 by Mary Myers

MARY McBRIDE

When it comes to writing romance, Mary McBride is a natural. What else would anyone expect from someone whose parents met on a blind date on Valentine's Day, and who met her own husband—whose middle name just happens to be Valentine—on February 14, as well?

In addition to her contemporary romances, she has also written eleven historical romances for Harlequin Historicals, most recently *Bandera's Bride*, a June 2000 release.

She lives in St. Louis, Missouri, with her husband and two sons. Mary loves to hear from readers. You can write to her c/o P.O. Box 411202, St. Louis, MO 63141.

IT'S OUR 20th ANNIVERSARY!
We'll be celebrating all year,
Continuing with these fabulous titles,
On sale in September 2000.

Intimate Moments

 #1027 Night Shield
Nora Roberts

#1028 Night of No Return
Eileen Wilks

 #1029 Cinderella for a Night
Susan Mallery

#1030 I'll Be Seeing You
Beverly Bird

#1031 Bluer Than Velvet
Mary McBride

#1032 The Temptation of Sean MacNeill
Virginia Kantra

Special Edition

 #1345 The M.D. She Had To Marry
Christine Rimmer

#1346 Father Most Wanted
Marie Ferrarella

#1347 Gray Wolf's Woman
Peggy Webb

#1348 For His Little Girl
Lucy Gordon

#1349 A Child on the Way
Janis Reams Hudson

#1350 At the Heart's Command
Patricia McLinn

Desire

 #1315 Slow Waltz Across Texas
Peggy Moreland

#1316 Rock Solid
Jennifer Greene

#1317 The Next Santini Bride
Maureen Child

#1318 Mail-Order Cinderella
Kathryn Jensen

#1319 Lady with a Past
Ryanne Corey

#1320 Doctor for Keeps
Kristi Gold

Romance

 #1468 His Expectant Neighbor
Susan Meier

 #1469 Marrying Maddy
Kasey Michaels

#1470 Daddy in Dress Blues
Cathie Linz

#1471 The Princess's Proposal
Valerie Parv

#1472 A Gleam in His Eye
Terry Essig

#1473 The Librarian's Secret Wish
Carol Grace

Chapter 1

"Most people hire a private investigator to *find* somebody, Miss McNeal. Not the other way around."

"Well, I'm not most people, Mr. Zachary."

"Yeah. I can see that."

What the man could see, Laura McNeal thought as she reversed the upward creep of her hemline and the downward plunge of her bodice, was plenty of cleavage and way too much leg, but she couldn't help that. There hadn't been time to change.

What *she* could see, on the other hand, was a dingy, pea soup-colored room with a scuffed linoleum floor and windows that were so dirty they barely let in more than a ray or two of daylight. Against one wall there was a dented metal filing cabinet. Against the other wall was a calendar with a picture of Rocky and Bullwinkle on top and the wrong month hanging down below.

The place looked more like the Salvation Army furniture annex than an office, and across the big battered desk, slouched a man who didn't look at all like a tough-as-nails private eye.

Just her luck. She'd been in the market for a German shepherd, rabid if possible, and she'd wound up with a Saint Bernard, instead. She needed Sam Spade, but who did she get? Sam Spoon.

"Mind if I ask how you got my number, Miss McNeal?"

"The phone book," she said, not adding that out of the dozen or so private investigators listed there, *Zachary, S. U.* was the very last one she had tried. Her first call that morning had been to Allied Investigators, but when she detailed her immediate problem for the man on the phone, he had made it absolutely clear that his agency didn't want to be allied with her *or* her problem.

All the other investigators she had called had been out of their offices, presumably plying their trade, and she had been too desperate to leave a message with a secretary or on an answering machine, too frightened to wait for someone who might or might not return her call.

Then, when she called Zachary, S. U., he answered his own phone. No secretary. That should have set off a little warning bell right then that maybe Zachary, S. U. wasn't the keenest private eye in town.

Laura remembered wondering what the initials S.U. stood for. Now she came to the unhappy conclusion that they probably stood for Seriously Unqualified. Or Severely Unemployed. Sexual Undercurrent also came fleetingly to mind, but she immediately dismissed that notion.

"And the shiner?" he asked.

Laura blinked, painfully. "Excuse me?"

"How'd you get the shiner?" He touched a finger to his eye. At the outer corner where the deep, sexy crinkles were. "You know. The black eye."

She wracked her Suddenly Unprepared brain for an answer that wouldn't unnerve this last-ditch detective as much as the truth had unnerved the first. If a real investigator didn't want to have anything to do with her even on the phone, this guy would probably pick her up bodily and throw her out of his office.

"I got it from the man I don't want to find me so he can do it again," she said as firmly as she could.

"Did you call the police? File a report?"

Laura just shook her head and tried to look pathetic, even more than she already did, so he wouldn't ask why she hadn't called the police. Nobody called the police about Art "the Hammer" Hammerman or his son, Artie, unless they had a particular fondness for black-and-blue or an incredible longing for plastic surgery or—worse—an outright death wish.

"I'd recommend that you do," he said. "File a report. The sooner the better."

"I'll think about it."

Laura never meant to cry, but all of a sudden a big tear plopped on the blue velvet of her skirt, followed quickly by another and another. She brushed at them, then brushed again to reverse the dark nap of the velvet, then just kept brushing, unable to stop either that or the stupid crying.

Oh, hell.

Sam Zachary yanked open the warped, top right

drawer of his secondhand desk. When he didn't see a box of tissues, he slammed the drawer shut and opened the top left, the middle left, then every other drawer. He had scratch pads, legal pads, an outdated phone book, a lifetime supply of paper clips and cheap ballpoint pens, four cans of tomato juice and half a dozen granola bars, but not a single tissue for this weeping woman. Dammit.

Then he heard the distinctive sound of a tissue being plucked from a box, and realized she had helped herself from the box hidden behind a stack of magazines and client files on the far side of his desk.

"I'm sorry," she blurted out between soggy sniffs. "I'll be fine. I really will. Just give me a minute to get myself together, will you?"

"Sure. Take your time."

Sam leaned back in his chair, battening down that natural instinct of his to wrap his arms around a crying female, especially this one in her ditzy little dress that left almost nothing to the imagination. Except that wasn't quite true because his imagination had gone into overdrive the minute she'd walked into his office a little after noon like a blond, blue velvet vision teetering on three-inch spiked, rhinestone-studded heels. With a shiner the size of Rhode Island.

He sighed softly. *Why me?*

Using his surname plus initials rather than some macho company name and batting last in the Yellow Pages had been a fairly successful strategy thus far in limiting his business. He really hated his job, and used any excuse not to do it. Today was the twentieth, and just as soon as he wrapped up the surveillance on Millard Boynton—straying spouse No. 72—

he planned to take the rest of the month off, add thirty or forty square feet to his vegetable garden, put in some good mileage on his rowing machine, and finally nail down Bach's "Jesu Joy of Man's Desiring" on the piano.

In a minute, once the waterworks stopped, Miss or Mrs. Laura McNeal was going to lift her blue velvet eyes from her blue velvet lap and ask him—no, she was going to implore him—to help her escape an abusive husband or, more likely, to elude an overly aggressive pimp.

Sam Zachary was already framing his reply.

No.

He hadn't gotten far beyond that thought when Miss or Mrs. Laura McNeal sniffed a conclusive sniff, wadded the soggy tissue in her fist, then recrossed her dynamite legs, and leaned forward.

"Will you help me, Mr. Zachary? Please. I need to disappear."

Sam felt his eyes snap up from the wisp of black lace just visible at the leading edge of her neckline.

"I'm not a magician," he said half-heartedly.

"Please."

"I'm pretty expensive," he said. *Coward.*

"How much?" She was already withdrawing a checkbook and a big blue fountain pen from a tiny beaded purse that didn't look as if it could hold more than a key and a Kleenex.

"A hundred dollars a day, plus expenses." *Liar. It's two-fifty and you know it.* He cleared his throat and shifted in his chair. The springs squealed like stuck pigs. "I'd need a hundred as an advance." *Instead of the usual five.*

"You've got it."

She wrote the check with a quick, left-handed flourish that struck Sam as a nearly impossible feat, then she ripped it out and waved it like a tiny flag of victory before she passed it across his desktop.

"So, what do we do first?" she asked. "I mean, to make me disappear?"

Sam closed his eyes a moment. That was one way of doing it, he thought.

For starters, Zachary, S. U. had told Laura that he was going to take her someplace safe. That had entailed a walk down the three flights of stairs from his office and then a pretty precarious climb into the front seat of his battered, black Chevy Blazer truck, which had also afforded S.U. not only a further glimpse of thigh but the opportunity to clamp his hand to her blue velvet backside when one of her high heels slipped off the running board.

Beside him now as he wove the vehicle through traffic, Laura asked, "So, what does the S.U. stand for?"

"Sam," he said, hitting the brakes for a sudden amber light. "Samuel Ulysses, actually."

"Oh, God." Laura rolled her eyes. He *was* a Sam, even if he wasn't Sam Spade. She started to giggle.

"What's so funny?"

"Nothing." The laughter she tried to stifle erupted in a snort. The facial contortion made her eye hurt. "It's just sort of a private joke."

He gave her a sidelong glance—a fairly withering one, in her estimation—then said, "Between you and yourself, I take it."

"Sort of." Laura sat up straighter, tugging her hemline down and her bodice up. "Sam's a nice name, actually. You should use it in the phone book instead of those silly initials.''

"I'll take that into consideration.''

He stepped on the gas, and Laura was pretty sure she saw his fingers tighten on the steering wheel and his mouth shape a tiny, impatient sneer. Oh, great. Her big Saint Bernard was turning out to be as irritable as a cocker spaniel. She sighed. This wasn't going to work.

"Look, maybe we should just forget...''

Sam Zachary spoke the exact words, at that exact moment, in the same frustrated tone of voice. A quick little grin telegraphed across his lips before he stiffened them again.

"I really do need some help,'' Laura said quietly, looking down while she traced a beaded daisy on her handbag, not daring to look at him because she didn't know whether or not she was going to dissolve into tears again. For someone who had barely shed a tear in the past decade, she was certainly making up for it now.

"I know,'' he answered just as quietly. "That's why I'm taking you someplace where you'll be safe.''

Safe. That was all she wanted to be just then. Safe from rotten Artie Hammerman.

Laura tilted her head back and closed her eyes, one of which had begun to throb painfully. Maybe it was all her fault. Maybe if she hadn't accepted Artie's first, surprising gift, none of this would have happened. But nobody had given her flowers since her senior prom, and suddenly, three weeks ago, there was her landlord's bullnecked, muscle-bound son, dressed in a checked suit with foot wide lapels and a tie as wide as the Mississippi River, angling a huge box of long-stemmed, deep red American Beauties through the front door of her shop.

"Oh, Artie," she'd exclaimed. "For me? They're beautiful. But why?"

Her next mistake was accepting his dopey shrug and big gooey smile as a satisfactory answer.

Then came the candy. She didn't even know they made heart-shaped boxes that big! Or bottles of Chanel No. 5 that were so enormous they had to be picked up with two hands.

After the perfume arrived, she got nervous and put in a call to the Hammer himself. But Art Hammerman, Sr., had brushed off her concerns about his son.

"Don't worry about it," he'd told her in that Don Corleone voice of his. "Indulge the kid."

But then the car came. A white convertible with red leather seats and the biggest red bow that Laura had ever seen. That had been early this morning, just before Artie knelt before her and opened the little hinged purple box with the big diamond ring nestled inside it.

Then, when she told him he had to take it back, Artie had pushed her, then pulled her, then finally punched her, all the while bellowing "If I can't have you, Laura, then nobody else can, either."

Well, nobody else wanted her. But that wasn't exactly the point. And nobody, by God, had ever hit her. Ever.

"What'd I do wrong?" she muttered now, dragging her fingers through her hair. "I really, really don't deserve this."

"People rarely do, Miss McNeal."

She'd almost forgotten that Zachary, S. U. was

sitting barely two feet away, his eyes safely glued to the road, his hands at a steady ten and two on the wheel. "Excuse me?"

"I said people rarely get what they deserve. Good, bad or indifferent."

Great, Laura thought. He was a philosopher, too.

"Well, they should," she answered irritably.

They were crossing the two-lane Tri-County Bridge just then. The river glittered below in the summer sun. Laura looked back. The steel-and-glass towers of the city were diminishing fast. Ahead of them, on both sides of the ribbon of road, stretched green fields, broken only by an occasional farmhouse and a dull red barn.

It suddenly occurred to Laura that it might be prudent to ask Sam Zachary just where he was taking her. Maybe this wasn't such a good idea. What if she had escaped rotten Artie Hammerman only to be abducted by a guy who sat in a crummy little office just waiting for innocent victims to come along? What if the *S* really stood for Serial, as in killer?

Laura swallowed hard. Then the *U* was obviously for Uh-oh.

She glanced to her left. Sam Zachary didn't look like a sociopath or a menace to society. He didn't even look dangerous. He looked…well…sincere. Even sweet. All this despite the fact that he also looked strong as an ox.

His thigh muscles bunched just under the faded denim of his jeans. His navy polo shirt curved across a barrel of a chest and the short sleeves showed off his tanned, muscular arms. The sweetness, though, was in the little upward curve of his mouth and the deep crinkles at the outer corners of his eyes. Actually, he was a very good-looking man.

But so was Ted Bundy.

"Do you have a license or anything?" she asked, breaking their silence.

Those lips tilted up a little bit more. "Good time to ask." He shifted in the seat, stretching out a long left leg, and produced a worn leather wallet from his back pocket.

"Here," he said, tossing it onto her lap.

Laura breathed a little easier after she opened it and saw not only his driver's license but a pretty official-looking license from the State Board of Private Investigators. Zachary, Samuel Ulysses was thirty-three, six foot three, and weighed two hundred and fifteen pounds. She already knew he had medium brown hair, although the card failed to mention that it was slightly sun-streaked, and that his brown eyes held an incredible warmth while they crinkled at the corners.

"Satisfied?" he asked, holding out an open hand for the return of his wallet.

Laura closed it and plopped it in his palm. "I guess so." Relieved was more like it, she thought. "Now I should probably ask where you're taking me."

No sooner were the words out of her mouth than he slowed the truck and hit the turn signal. "We're almost there," he said, turning the big Blazer left onto a shaded and narrow gravel road.

Laura's first thought was that this was probably the rural equivalent of a dark, deserted alley, that proverbial place where you never wanted to meet anybody, but before she was able to feel properly hysterical, she found herself quite overwhelmed by the beauty of the scene.

Big trees along both sides of the road formed a green, sun-dappled canopy high overhead, and through the trees to her right Laura could see a pasture brightly carpeted with wildflowers where horses and cows were grazing contentedly. A white wooden fence ran along the edge of the road, and birds—blue ones and red ones and black ones with red-spotted wings—perched atop every other fence post as if they'd been hired by a landscaper for decorating duty.

"This is lovely," she said, opening the window all the way and sticking her head out to take in a deep breath of the fresh, clean country air. "I haven't been out here in years. I'm pretty much a city girl."

She sighed as she edged down the hemline that had crept several inches up her thigh when she leaned out the window, and just for good measure she gave her bodice an upward tug. "You can probably tell."

"I can tell." Now he swung the car into another, narrower canopied lane, then put on the brakes in front of one of the most enchanting Victorian houses that Laura had ever seen.

It was two stories of pristine white clapboard and dark green shutters, of spooled archways and gingerbread eaves, all of it nestled into a deep wraparound porch. There was a porch swing with dark green cushions. Oh, and a trellis fairly groaning with bright yellow roses in the sideyard, and not too far from that a wonderful blue gazing ball that mirrored the entire, incredible scene.

"Oh, this is just absolutely gorgeous! I love it!"

Laura exclaimed. "What is it? A bed and breakfast?"

"Nope." Sam Zachary turned off the ignition and plucked out the key. "It's home," he said. "Come on."

Sam went into the kitchen after doing a quick inspection of the rest of the house. The important rooms—the living room, guest room, and both baths—looked fairly decent, much to his relief. It had been a while since he'd had anybody in to clean. Although why he was worrying about Laura McNeal's first impression of his house was beyond him.

On the drive from the city, he'd pretty well concluded that she was a hooker. She had to be. Nobody else would dress that way in the middle of the day. Nobody else would dress that way *period.*

He'd left her on the porch swing, happy as a three-year-old, smiling while she pushed the big wooden swing back and forth with the pointed toes of her impossibly high, rhinestone-studded heels. She struck him as unusually carefree for a working girl who was obviously out of work for the duration.

Unless she thought that he...

Sam had just opened the refrigerator door, but now he slammed it shut. He must be nuts, bringing this woman here. It had seemed so obvious, so perfect. An ideal hideout where he could keep a casual watch out for her while carrying on with his own life. What was he thinking?

Shaking his head, he opened the door again and grabbed two cans of diet cola. She was still blissfully swinging when he walked out on the porch. Fine host that he was, he popped the tab on her cola before he handed it to her.

"We need to talk, Miss McNeal. We need to get a few things clear." He slung a hip up on the porch rail, staring down at her, blatantly ignoring her long shapely legs and world-class ankles. "It is Miss, isn't it?"

"Why don't you just call me Laura?"

"Okay, Laura. But that still doesn't answer my question. Are you single? Married?"

"Single," she replied, and Sam felt a sudden, inexplicable, almost goofy sense of relief. He immediately relegated it to the fact that he didn't like working domestic disputes which tended to be ugly if not downright dangerous. People who loved each other could be the very worst of enemies.

"So you're not trying to get away from an angry husband, then, I guess."

"No."

Sam sighed. He felt more like a dentist pulling teeth than a P.I. eliciting details from a client. "Who, then?"

"A man."

He stared out at the yard a moment, courting patience, taking a break from the sight of her lovely legs. "You're going to have to be a bit more specific, Miss, uh, Laura," he finally said, "if you want me to help you with this situation."

"A man who wants to marry me even though he barely knows me."

Okay. So she wasn't running away from her pimp. That still didn't mean she wasn't a hooker. One of her johns got emotionally involved no doubt. Somehow that didn't surprise Sam. Laura McNeal was a beautiful woman. She had a face like an angel and a body custom-designed for sin. His own body, as a matter of fact, was acutely aware of hers at the moment. He took a swig from the soda can in the hope of cooling off.

"This man," he said. "He's a john, I assume."

"No," she answered, after a quick, confused blink. "He's an Artie."

Then it was Sam's turn to blink. "Excuse me?"

She kicked off one shoe, then the other, and tucked about six miles of slender leg beneath her. "The man who hit me, the one who wants to marry me, is named Artie."

"I meant, is he one of your customers?"

She shook her head, frowning. "No. Artie's never..." Then her velvety blue eyes sparked with sudden comprehension. "That kind of john!" she exclaimed. "You think I'm a...a prostitute?"

"Well, I... You know." He gestured to her minuscule dress and the discarded shoes. "The clothes and all."

The swing started to rock back and forth with her laughter. "Oh, Sam. That is *so* funny. You thought I was a prostitute!"

He glowered now, feeling foolish, not to mention pretty inept in the deductive reasoning department, and nearly shouted, "Well, why the hell else would you wear a getup like that?"

"Because I own a vintage clothing store, that's why."

Sam thought she might have ended with "you idiot" but he wasn't sure because, laughing as hard as she was, Laura could hardly get the words out clearly.

"This…" She touched the skimpy skirt of the dress. "…is because I was trying on some new merchandise when Artie showed up this morning. Then, after he hit me, I was out of there. I didn't take time to change."

"That was smart," he said, hoping the praise would make her forget that he'd insulted her.

"Not smart so much as scared. Especially when he said, 'If I can't have you, then nobody else will, either.'"

Sam didn't like the sound of that one bit, but he didn't want to frighten this woman more than she already was. "And you think he means it?"

"I know he means it." She touched her bruised eye, wincing slightly. "Oh, boy, does he mean it."

"Artie what? What's this creep's last name?"

For an instant, she looked blank. Then her lips compressed and her gaze cut away from his for the briefest moment before coming back. "Jones," she said. "The creep's name is Artie Jones."

Sam nodded and murmured, "Okay," then took a long and thoughtful sip of his cola, all the while wondering why this woman felt compelled to lie to him—and badly, too—about her assailant's name. And if that was a lie, he wondered just how much else about Laura McNeal he should allow himself to believe.

Chapter 2

Oh, good one, Laura!

Jones! She felt like smacking the heel of her hand to her forehead. If she intended to make up a different surname for Artie, couldn't she at least have come up with something a little bit more original? Jones! She might as well have said Smith. The only thing the fake name had going for it was that she'd probably be able to remember it if Sam Zachary asked her again.

He probably would, too. She was sure of that. The private investigator had gone a little thin-lipped and slit-eyed when she'd answered his question, but there was no way on earth she was going to tell him the truth when the mere mention of the name Hammerman tended to make people sweat and develop uncontrollable tics. Even people as big as Sam Zachary.

For every one of his reputable businesses, Art "the Hammer" Hammerman probably had two or three disreputable ones. He was a landlord whose buildings often inexplicably burned down. He was a land developer whose notion of eminent domain included threats, poisoning family pets, and if necessary a well-aimed rifle shot through a kitchen window. A labor leader who had an endless supply of thugs to do his bidding and just enough cops and judges so he never got caught, or if caught, he certainly never went to jail.

But worst of all right now in Laura's view, the Hammer had a son who wouldn't take no for an answer.

She was following Sam into the house now after he'd told her it would be a good idea if she stayed here at least for a day or two until he could come up with a more suitable plan. That had sounded reasonable to Laura. She was even relaxing a bit, having come to the conclusion that if Sam had intended to assault and rape her, the man had already had ample opportunity and hadn't made even a remotely devious or lecherous move. At least none that she was aware of.

Anyway, she wanted to stay.

The inside of the house turned out to be even more inviting than the exterior. The ancient hardwood floors had been lovingly cared for. So had the lace curtains at the windows, although they did look as if they could use a quick little dip in some bleach. There was a Victorian sofa with a carved mahogany back and fabulous claw feet, which was heaped with at least a dozen plump tapestry and needlepoint pillows into which Laura could've done an immediate swan dive.

Everywhere she looked were wonderful knickknacks and gewgaws and bits of kitsch. They sat on shelves, on crocheted doilies atop tables, on the antique what-not in the corner. Paperweights and porcelain figures. Vases and glass animals and Kewpie dolls. They marched across the mantel and formed chorus lines on all the windowsills. It was a collector's paradise.

"I feel like I've died and gone to heaven," Laura heard herself saying. "Look at all this magnificent stuff!"

Sam, with one foot already on the bottom step of a staircase, came to a standstill, then slowly turned to face her. "What? All this junk?"

"It's not junk," she said, almost indignantly. "What a marvelous place. It's like living in…"

He snorted, interrupting her. "Secondhand Charlie's Garage and Used Furniture Outlet."

Laura shook her head. "No." Her voice sounded disembodied, almost dreamy, even to her. "No, it's like living in my Nana's house. It's perfect."

"Perfect," he muttered. "You're kidding, right?"

She shook her head again. "It's wonderful, Sam. How long have you lived here?"

"All my life."

Edging back one sheer lacy curtain, Laura lifted a small white pot of violets from the sill and inspected its five, no, six deep purple blooms. She had a sudden vision of her grandmother's fingers, stiff with arthritis and freckled with age, poking into the soil below the dark, velvety leaves of African violets. She could almost hear Nana's chirpy voice. *Don't let their little feet dry out, Laura, honey.*

Only then did she notice that there was moisture in the saucer attached to the pot. Sam Zachary, Private Eye, watered African violets! Why that pleased her so much, Laura couldn't have said. It was just…well…sweet somehow and far more domestic than she ever would have given him credit for, especially considering his ratty, run-down office in the city.

"You should probably feed this little guy, too," she said almost to herself, putting the pot back on the sill, then turning to the man who was waiting for her at the foot of the stairs. "All your life here. What a lucky, lucky man you are."

Sam started up the stairs, listening to each familiar groan and creak, testing the give in the banister, thinking that he'd never felt like a lucky, lucky man. Ever. Well, not lately anyway. Not since Jenny Sayles's car had slid through a guardrail on Highway A-14 and then crashed in the icy underbrush along Cabin Creek. When Jenny died, all his luck, both good and bad, had perished with her, and Sam had lived in a sort of luckless limbo ever since.

He turned left at the top of the stairs, then opened the door of the spare room which his mother had also used as a sewing room. The clutter inside rivaled that of the living room downstairs. Laura McNeal ought to be in hog heaven up here, he thought.

"This should be fairly comfortable," he told her. "As far as I know, the bed's hardly ever been slept in."

She made a beeline for his mother's ancient Singer sewing machine, still parked on a card table, and ran a hand over its worn black surface. He'd seen women look at diamonds or fur coats the same way, their eyes a little glazed, their faces touched with an ineffable longing. But a sewing machine? Sam was half tempted to tell her to take the damned thing with her when she left, but then he was leery of whatever form her expression of gratitude might take.

"Well, I'll just let you get settled in," he said. "Bathroom's just on the right. I won't be in your way."

"Thanks. I'll try to keep out of your way, too."

"Don't worry about it. I'm going to go take a look in the freezer and see if I have a nice little steak I can thaw out."

"I really don't expect you to feed me, too," she said.

Sam lifted his index finger to touch his eye. "A medicinal steak."

"Oh. Does that really work?"

"Couldn't hurt."

He winked at her as he stepped back into the hall, and then descended the stairs muttering to himself. Winking! Good God. He *never* winked. Guys in polyester suits with gold chains around their necks winked. So he convinced himself it was just a sympathetic twitch, brought on no doubt from the pitiful sight of the woman's purple shiner.

Laura only meant to test the bed. She woke up three hours later, startled at first by her strange surroundings, then comforted by the sight of the sewing machine. She stretched beneath the soft warmth of the granny afghan, then stopped midstretch, suddenly realizing that Sam Zachary must have come in and covered her with it while she was sleeping.

The Big Ben clock on the nightstand told her it was almost six o'clock. Her stomach reminded her that she hadn't eaten since Artie Hammerman smashed his fist into her half eaten glazed doughnut this morning just before he'd smashed it into her face. She lay there for a moment, refusing to even contemplate her predicament, while from somewhere downstairs came the clattering of pots and pans and the metallic rattling of silverware and the occasional thud of a refrigerator door.

She smelled coffee, too, and lay there imagining the beguiling fragrance wafting up the staircase like wavy banners in a cartoon. Her stomach growled. Hadn't Sam Zachary said something about a steak?

For lack of a comb, she ran her fingers through her hair, at the same time deciding not to get anywhere near the oval mirror above the antique dresser for fear of sending herself into a deep depression. If her eye looked anything like it felt, which was awful, she didn't even want to see it.

Laura had trotted halfway down the staircase, still listening to kitchen noises, when it suddenly occurred to her that it might not be Sam Zachary who was making all that decidedly domestic racket. He had inquired about her marital status, she recalled, but she hadn't asked him if he was married, had she? Instead she'd just assumed—maybe even vaguely hoped—he wasn't.

"Stupid," she muttered, wrenching her tight skirt into line and tucking in her chin to check for any undue exposure. She did the best she could to disguise her cleavage, then sighed. It probably didn't matter. As a private investigator's wife, Mrs. Sam Zachary had no doubt seen her share of weirdos and woebegone people. Laura was feeling a bit of both when she reached the bottom of the stairs and turned left, past the dining room, in order to search out the kitchen.

Sam was standing at the sink, his back to the door while his wide shoulders almost blocked out the light from the blue gingham-curtained window. Gingham apron strings from a big floppy bow in the center of his back dangled over his decidedly iron buns. Sam Zachary in an apron! If there was a Mrs. Zachary, Laura thought, the woman definitely belonged in the matrimonial hall of fame.

"Hey," she said, stepping into the room.

"Hey." He turned sideways just enough to give her a glimpse of the ruffles on the apron's bib. "You fell asleep."

"I know. I'm sorry. I didn't plan to."

"No problem. Are you hungry?"

"Famished."

"Good," he said. "You're in charge of the salad." He picked up a white plastic colander and held it out in her direction. "The garden's out the back door to the left. There are tomatoes and onions and radishes, a couple of early peppers, and maybe even some endive left."

Laura grasped the colander, trying not to let her expression betray the fact that she hadn't the vaguest idea what endive looked like. Especially on the hoof, so to speak. Jeez. Didn't they have supermarkets around here?

"Back in a jiffy," she said as she pushed open the screen door and stepped outside where she inhaled a long draught of the clean country air ever-so-slightly tinged with roses. It was nice, she thought, not to breathe bus fumes and three-day-old garbage. She was going to enjoy this little vacation.

The well-tended, rectangular garden was easy enough to find, even though her three-inch heels had an annoying tendency to sink into the ground. She pulled two red tomatoes from a tall vine, then bent forward and plucked a little clump of leaves from the dark soil.

"What do you know? A radish!" she murmured, shaking off some of the dirt before plopping it into the plastic bowl and proceeding to pick several more of its mates. The onions weren't all that difficult to identify, and she tugged up four of those. Then she straightened up and gave the rest of the garden the once-over, searching for the mysterious endive.

Spying something green with curly leaves on the far side of the little plot, she made her way on tiptoe around a pinwheeling plastic sunflower and several wire cages. Then—"Oh, please, please, don't let this be anything poisonous."—she reached down to pluck a leaf just as something sprang up into her face.

She jerked upright. The thing, the horrible thing, was in her hair, so she batted at it, only to have the creature take a flying leap down the front of her dress.

Then Laura did what any normal, self-respecting city girl would do. She screamed bloody murder.

Sam dropped the potato peeler in the sink, picked up the 12-gauge shotgun behind the back door, and was out in the backyard in mere seconds expecting to find his client fighting for her very life with a bruiser named Artie. Instead she was hopping around the back of the garden, flapping the front of her dress, screaming "Get it off me! Get it off me!"

He put the gun down in the grass and headed toward the garden, trying to wipe off the grin that he knew would only irritate her.

"Get it off me," she shrieked as he neared.

"Hold still."

Apparently she couldn't, so he grasped her shoulders, turning her toward him. "Will you hold still? It's probably just a grasshopper. It's not going to hurt you."

"Get. It. Off." Her eyes squinched closed in her already squinched face.

"Okay. Okay."

He looked at her hair and scanned the blue velvet on her shoulders and neckline. "I don't see anything. It must've taken off."

"It's down my dress," she said.

"Down..." Sam's gaze dropped to the pale skin bordered by a hint of black lace. "I can't..."

"Get it," she shrieked.

"Hold still."

He closed his own eyes a second, letting out a kind of heaven-help-me sigh, then eased his fingers into the front of the dress, down into black lace and blue velvet and warm, firm flesh. Lucky little guy, he thought, as he gently pinched the ends of a pair of frantic wings, then eased the insect as well as himself up and out. The grasshopper shot away in a single, ecstatic leap.

"You can open your eyes now," Sam said.

She did, but just barely. "I *hate* bugs."

Sam retrieved the colander that Laura had apparently flung off into space when she was attacked, and now he was picking up scattered vegetables and at the same time trying not to think about the heat his hand had so recently encountered beneath all that blue velvet. He started to say something, but she sliced him with a glare.

"And don't you dare say they're more afraid of me than I am of them, Sam Zachary, because it isn't true."

"I wasn't going to say that," Sam said, reaching to break off a few tender leaves of endive and laying them on top of the tomatoes and radishes and green onions. "I was only going to ask you how you like your steak and what kind of dressing you prefer on your salad."

"Oh." She gave a little shrug. "Medium, I guess, and Thousand Island. French would be fine, too."

"Okay."

He shouldn't have asked, Sam thought, since he had every intention of grilling the rib eye black on the outside and a perfect, medium-rare pink inside, and tossing the salad with a tarragon vinaigrette.

All of a sudden he felt irritable, curmudgeonly, like a doddering old bachelor too set in his ways to even listen to anyone else's preferences. Or worse. Too comfortable with the familiar to appreciate something new and different. Some*one* new and different.

"Better get back inside," he grumbled, "before the praying mantises start to swarm." He handed her the colander. "Here. Take this. I need to get my shotgun."

She shivered. "Not for the praying mantises, I hope."

"No." He picked up the gun. "I only use this on the wolf spiders."

* * *

"You were kidding, right, about the wolf spiders?" Laura asked halfway through dinner.

They were sitting in the kitchen on opposite sides of what she considered a very retro aluminum-and-plastic dinette set. The whole room, in fact, was fabulously retro. It looked as if it had been lifted from another era with its white metal cabinets, its fake marble linoleum floor, and almost boxcar-sized white enamel stove.

"Yes, I was kidding," Sam answered with a subdued little chuckle. "How's your steak?"

"Fabulous." She took another mouthwatering bite. "It would've been a waste to use it on my eye. The salad's great, too. You made the dressing yourself?"

He nodded.

Sam Zachary was still wearing his apron, but the blue gingham and ruffles couldn't make even the slightest dent in his masculinity. In an odd way, Laura decided, they seemed to accentuate it all the more. God, he was gorgeous. Not that that was any big deal. Not that she cared.

"So, where'd you learn to cook, Zachary, S. U.?" she asked, putting her knife and fork down to pick up the cold bottle of beer he'd put at her place.

"Right here. After my mother died last year, it was a case of either learning how to cook for myself or wasting away to skin and bones."

Laura nodded. She knew what that was like. She'd been in a similar situation a few years before when her grandmother passed away, but she'd solved the skin-and-bones problem with pizza deliveries and salad bars and take-out Chinese.

"I meant what I said, Sam. About not having to feed me. I'm sure I'm not paying you enough for…"

"I'll put it on your tab," he said, pushing his empty plate away, then taking a swig from his own bottle of beer. He put the dark brown bottle down, returning it precisely to the wet circle it had made on the tabletop, before he leaned back and crossed his arms. "You want to tell me a little bit more about this Jones guy so I have a better idea what I'm dealing with?"

"Jones?"

"The slugger?" He gestured to her eye.

"Oh. *That* Jones."

She shifted in her chair, but the vinyl seat had such a good grip on her thighs, it felt as if she'd ripped off a layer of skin. It didn't help, either, that she could almost hear Nana chanting *Oh, what a tangled web we weave.*

"Artie, you mean."

He gave her a long, silent, steely-eyed stare which seemed to translate as yes, that was exactly what he meant and not to confuse the blue gingham apron with a blue gingham disposition.

"Artie's, um, well…persistent," she said.

"How long have you been seeing him?"

Laura blinked. "Seeing him?"

"Dating him," Sam clarified.

"Dating Artie?" She almost laughed, then shook her head. "No, you don't understand. I've never gone out with him. He's my landlord's son and for some reason he's been giving me presents the past few weeks. Flowers. Candy. Stuff like that. I thought it was, well, kind of cute in the beginning." She reached out, tracing a finger along the label of her beer bottle, frowning now. "It stopped being cute this morning."

"So you've never gone out with him?"

"Never. Not once. Come to think of it, he never even asked me out." She quit staring at the label and lifted her eyes to Sam's. "Pretty weird, huh?"

More than weird, Sam was thinking. He could well imagine, once having met Laura McNeal, wanting to shower her with gifts, but he couldn't fathom not asking her out on a date, as well. Unless, of course, this Artie guy knew that she was already involved with somebody else. If she was, though, why hadn't she gone to that somebody else for help?

"Do you live alone?" he asked her, not quite hitting the target of his curiosity dead-on, but edging close.

She nodded. "I live in an apartment over my shop."

"Your shop?"

"I told you. Remember?" She gestured to her dress. "I have a vintage clothing and jewelry store. Nana's Attic."

"Ah." He *had* forgotten, which didn't say a lot for his ability to process information at the moment. He wanted to blame the beer, but he knew it was that damned grasshopper down the front of Laura's dress. The backs of his fingers still felt warm from their brief contact with her flesh.

Abruptly, he picked up his empty plate and carried it to the sink.

"I've got a job tonight," he said over his shoulder, over the splash of the water from the faucet. "I need to drive back into the city around midnight. Just for a few hours. You can stay here if you want. You'll be safe. But if you feel uncomfortable, you can come along with me. It's up to you.''

"What kind of job?'' She picked up her plate, too, and headed toward him at the sink.

Sam had forgotten about her legs during dinner while those long and lovely limbs were concealed beneath the table. He remembered them now, so vividly he almost forgot what she had just asked him. Oh, yeah. The job.

"Surveillance,'' he said. "It shouldn't take more than an hour or two.''

One of her finely shaped eyebrows arched a bit more. Her blue eyes twinkled and a smile played at her mouth. "Ooh, surveillance. Sounds dangerous. Real private eye stuff, huh?''

"Right.'' He took her plate and rinsed it under the faucet. "But it's not dangerous. Don't worry.''

"Oh, I wasn't worried. It's kind of exciting, actually. Who are we spying on? A murderer returning to the scene of his crime? A robber casing a bank? A big drug deal?''

"Not quite.''

"Well, what then?''

She was standing so close that he could see tiny golden flecks in the blue of her eyes as well as the true line of her lips, even fuller than her pink lipstick implied. A mouth made for kissing if ever he had seen one. Suddenly his brain was ticking off the months it had been since he'd kissed a woman. Not just a woman. Jenny. He'd really never kissed anyone else.

"You've seen too many movies,'' Sam said more gruffly than he intended, slapping their dishes and utensils into the dishwasher. "We're going to sit on a hot, tarred rooftop adjacent to the parking garage of the Metropole Hotel, waiting for a sixty-six-year-old man to finish his weekly tryst with his twenty-year-old receptionist, then watch him walk her to her car and kiss her good-night.''

"That doesn't sound too exciting," Laura said.

"Told ya." He wiped his hands on one of his mother's cross-stitched dishtowels and returned it to its metal bar beside the sink.

"And then?" she asked. "What happens next? You call the police and have him arrested?"

"Nope. Then I take a picture of the lovers, have it developed, and I give the print to a sweet little old lady with blue hair who's still ninety-nine percent convinced that her husband of forty-two years is playing gin rummy every Wednesday night."

The playful light in Laura's eyes went out like two candles being snuffed, and for a second, Sam regretted his candor.

"Well, you asked," he said. "Cases like that are the bulk of my work. Rescuing dames in distress is just a sideline."

He had hoped she'd laugh at that, lame as it was, but she didn't. Suddenly she looked less like a dame in distress than a sad little girl, playing dress up in her mother's clothes.

Reaching out, she straightened the dishtowel on its rod, then sighed. "You're right. It's not like the movies."

"You don't have to come along, you know. You really will be all right here if you want to stay."

She shook her head. "I'll just stick with you for a while, if you don't mind."

"I don't mind. It'll be nice to have company. Only…"

"Only what?"

"Well, the last time I saw a private eye's assistant dressed like this…" He dropped his gaze to the soft drapery of blue velvet sloping from her delicate collarbone. "…it *was* in a movie. Maybe there's something in one of the closets upstairs that might be a little bit less, um…"

"Vintage?" she suggested, the twinkle returning to her eyes.

"That, too." Sam stepped away from the sink, blaming the current spike in his temperature on all that humidity from the hot rinse water. "Come on. Let's have a look."

Sam leaned against the wall outside his mother's bedroom, listening to the distinctive sounds of a woman dressing and undressing, to the slide of hangers across a metal rod, the slithering of fabrics over skin, the puttings on and the peelings off, the snapping of snaps and the long glide of zippers opening and closing.

When he'd suggested that Laura might find something to wear in his late mother's closet, he hadn't expected her search to take so long, much less to take on the proportions of a Broadway production number. He needed to get back to the city to set up his surveillance.

"Are you about done in there?" he asked through the crack in the door.

"Just about," Laura called out, her voice slightly muffled by what sounded like crisp taffeta. "How long ago did you say your mother passed away?"

"Last year." He heard more rustling, more zipping or unzipping before she spoke again.

"White Shoulders," she said.

"Pardon?"

"Her fragrance. She wore White Shoulders, didn't she?"

Did she? Sam didn't have a clue, and he said so just as Laura suddenly appeared in the doorway.

"Some detective you are," she said, coming out into the hall while adjusting the shoulders and the neckline of her dress, which, to Sam's amazement, just happened to be the same, skimpy blue velvet getup she'd been wearing all day.

"I thought you were going to change," he said. "What happened? Didn't anything fit?"

"Just about everything fit."

"Well, what then?"

She was quiet a moment, standing with her hands on her hips and staring down at the floor. Then she sighed and gave a small shrug. "I don't want you to get the wrong idea, Sam, when I tell you. Promise me you won't, okay?"

"The wrong idea? About what?" he snapped.

"Don't be so angry."

"I'm not angry," he said, sounding more baffled now than angry. "I've just been hanging out here listening to you try on enough outfits to clothe the female population of a small city. And then, after all that, you come out in…" He stabbed a finger at her dress. "…in *this*."

"*This*," she said, jutting her chin into his face, "doesn't smell like White Shoulders."

"So?"

"So?" Her volume increased to match, if not

drown out, his. "So, if it's all right with you, Sam Zachary, I just didn't want to smell like your mother."

She flounced past him to stomp down the stairs, as much as anyone could stomp in stiletto heels, leaving Sam standing there shaking his head and wondering why it made any difference who she smelled like when he had no intention of getting close enough to tell.

And even if he did get close enough, say, to kiss her, there was no way he was ever going to confuse Laura McNeal with his mother.

Chapter 3

It was good to be back in the city, Laura thought. Well, sort of. If you didn't mind climbing six flights of smelly, littered stairs in a dark abandoned building, then camping out on a scratchy army blanket flung out on a hot, tarred roof where shards of broken liquor bottles glittered in the summer moonlight.

She wasn't complaining, though. Not out loud, anyway. Not even when her heels had stuck fast and deep in soft tar bubbles and Sam Zachary had to pick her up and carry her across the roof and then go back to retrieve her captured shoes. She didn't complain aloud even when the army blanket beneath her began to feel as if it was deliberately clawing at the backs of her thighs and calves. Not even when she decided she was about to die of thirst.

Eyeing the big canvas bag that Sam had brought with him and parked on a corner of the blanket, she asked, "You don't happen to have a can of soda or a water bottle in there, do you?"

He was sitting beside her as he had been for the past hour or so, knees drawn up, arms looped casually over them, and his gaze trained permanently on the cement maze of the parking garage next door. "Sorry."

Laura made a dry little noise deep in her throat, then ran her fingers through the damp locks of her hair, wondering vaguely if she might be able to lick some of that moisture from her hands. "It must be ninety degrees up here," she said, hoping he'd take the not-so-subtle hint.

"Probably."

"Definitely." Laura shifted on the blanket, letting it take a bite out of her right thigh now that it had pretty much chewed up her left.

Now, too late, she wished that she had changed into one of Sam's mother's outfits, regardless of their ingrained fragrance. Maybe the light blue pincord suit with its boxy jacket and long A-line skirt. Or maybe the navy piqué dress with the delicate lace collar. Both had fit her perfectly.

But, while she was trying on the garments, Laura had come to the conclusion that his mother's lingering scent would only make Sam sad, and she had decided that she'd rather keep looking inappropriate, if not bizarre, than cause this man a single moment of heartache. He had such a nice smile. Well, when he wasn't frowning.

She glanced over at him. In the moonlight his expression seemed neutral at the moment, neither happy nor sad. Just patient. As patient as a stone. He reminded her of the Sphinx, which reminded her of the desert, which reminded her of just how thirsty she was.

"I'd kill for a big, tall glass of iced tea," she said, trying not to whine, but following up her words with a pathetic little moan she couldn't suppress. "I guess you just forgot to bring anything to drink, huh?"

"I didn't forget," he said, still staring at the garage.

Laura immediately perked up. "Oh. You brought something, then?"

"No."

"But you said…"

"I said I didn't forget." His gaze cut toward her briefly before returning to the garage where the suspects' cars, a big silver boat of a Cadillac and a spiffy little red Toyota, were parked affectionately side by side. The vehicles hadn't moved, Laura noted glumly. Nor had the garage. Nor Sam.

What a crummy, boring occupation. She was seriously beginning to wonder if she'd made a mistake choosing Zachary, S. U. to protect her. In spite of his incredibly muscular build and sensational tan, he didn't strike her as a man of action exactly, or as all that smart and well prepared. If he had known they'd be spending half the night on a red-hot rooftop, why in heaven's name hadn't he at least thought to bring along something to drink? Even a thermos of luke-warm coffee or hot chocolate didn't sound half bad at the moment. A dented canteen with one swallow of anything wet.

"Pretty stupid, if you ask me," she muttered.

"What?"

"Not bringing anything to drink."

"No. Actually it's pretty smart," he said calmly.

"You don't see any bathroom facilities around here, do you?"

She glanced around the bleak rooftop. "No. No facilities whatsoever. Just half an acre of tar bubbles and broken glass."

"Well, there you go." He glanced at his watch. "It shouldn't be too much longer now. We'll stop on the way home for something."

"Mm." She had a vision of a foot tall glass of iced tea with a huge wedge of lemon stuck to its rim. "Be still my heart. I think I could drink a gallon of anything wet with ice cubes floating…"

"Shh." Sam cut off her liquid reverie with an abrupt hiss. And when Laura started to speak again, he growled, "Quiet. Somebody's coming."

As soon as he said that, Laura could hear the insistent bass of a boom box coming from the direction of the stairs. The noise became louder and louder until Laura could feel the rap music beginning to beat in her brain like a headache. Then the door to the rooftop opened, and two dark figures emerged.

Boys, she thought with a quick, small measure of relief. They were just kids. But as they sauntered closer, even in the dark Laura could see that both boys were decked in the obligatory ripped T-shirts, baggy, low-slung pants and turned-around baseball caps of the Devil's Own, one of the worst street gangs in the city. Worst as in cutthroat dangerous.

"Sorry, fellas," Sam called out above the harsh beat of the boom box. "This roof's occupied."

The boys stopped. So did the music. The sudden silence almost made Laura dizzy.

"Occupied," the taller one said to his companion. "*Occupied.*" He set the boom box down with exquisite care. "Maybe this man don't know what part of town he's occupying, Jerome."

"Damn straight," Jerome said gruffly as he jabbed a finger toward Sam and Laura. "This is our roof, man. We the Devil's Own."

They were also higher than any rooftop was ever going to get them, Laura noticed now from their slurred speech and unsteady stances. Their gazes, however, seemed to focus fairly steadily and unfortunately on her.

"Yo, mama," the tall, lanky one purred, smiling almost viciously as he took several easy steps in her direction. "Why don't you tell your old man there to take a hike for a little bitty while?"

She started to answer when Sam grasped her knee and said, "Just be quiet, Laura. Let me take care of this."

"Low-ra." Jerome turned the bill of his cap to the side, cocked his head, and grinned. Moonlight glittered on one big gold tooth. "You're one fine lady, Low-ra. Tell that sad-ass man of yours you want to stay here on that blanket with Swat and me. What do you say, Low-ra?"

She was tempted to say that she was a special friend of the Hammer's baby boy and if anything happened to her, they'd find themselves in a hundred various pieces scattered in dumpsters and vacant lots all over the city. Only her throat was so dry, all she could manage was to croak to Sam, "Don't you have a gun or something?"

"They're just kids," Sam said quietly. "I'm not going to pull a gun on kids."

But even as he was speaking, it seemed that the kids, Jerome and Swat, had decided they were not at all reluctant to use their own lethal weapons. First Jerome's long-bladed knife appeared from somewhere underneath his loose T-shirt. Then Swat's knife materialized, almost from thin air.

"Go on now, man," Jerome said, gesturing with the glinting blade. "We got some business with your lady."

Sam muttered a curse under his breath, then slowly began to get up. Laura's first thought was that he was going to do just what he'd been ordered to do, that he was going to walk away and leave her alone. Alone with the Devil's Own for *some business*. Panic surged up in her throat.

"Sam! What are you doing?" She reached out, grabbing for his pant leg, but he pulled away.

"Okay, fellas," he said. "Look, you really don't want to do this. Now put the knives away, pick up your boom box, and get the hell out of here before this gets you both a couple of years in Bakerville."

Laura felt her eyes rolling up in her head now, hardly believing what she'd just heard. These thugs were standing there with knives the size of machetes and Sam Zachary was threatening them with reform school! My God. At least he wasn't still wearing his blue gingham apron!

She decided right then and there that, after she survived this night, *if* she survived, she was going to find herself a real private investigator. A he-man. A hero. One with a very big gun.

Jerome and Swat, it appeared, had the same impression of Sam's abilities. They grinned at each other, traded knowing looks and began to move forward, one of them edging to the right and the other to the left.

"Two against one, man," Swat said, shifting his weapon from hand to hand and moving closer. "You scared yet?"

Plenty, Laura thought. Spitless.

"Terrified," Sam answered with a calmness that struck Laura as irrational, if not completely insane, under the circumstances.

Now the lanky Jerome started to make kissing noises. At least that's what Laura assumed they were. She didn't even want to know what the noises from Swat's mouth signified. Oh, God. This is what she'd escaped rotten Artie Hammerman for?

She glanced frantically toward the low brick wall that edged the rooftop, wondering just how much damage a sixty-foot jump might incur, thinking absurdly that if this were a movie there would be a series of canvas awnings to slow her fall, not to mention a conveniently parked truck with a flatbed of straw or stacked mattresses to keep her from breaking every bone in her body.

But this wasn't a movie and the two gang members were even closer to Sam now. One to the right, the other to the left. Close enough for Jerome to thrust out his blade in a wide, glittering and deadly arc.

What happened next took place so fast that Laura wasn't even sure her eyes completely registered the events. Sam's right arm shot out, deflecting the blade, then only a blink of an eye after that his left fist thundered into Jerome's chin, sending the boy at least half a foot into the air, literally out of his shoes. The knife went sailing, hilt over blade, into the moonlit sky, and before either Jerome or his weapon even had a chance to land, Sam's right fist smashed into Swat's face.

For a moment after that everything was absolutely quiet. Jerome sprawled on his back, motionless, three feet from his empty shoes. Swat knelt, his knees sunk deep in tar bubbles, his knife nowhere in sight, and blood from his broken nose pouring between his fingers.

Sam stood there for a moment, silently looking from boy to boy, flexing both hands, before he muttered a curse and turned toward Laura. To her amazement, he wasn't even breathing hard, and still looked cool and collected, as if he'd merely swatted a pair of pesky houseflies rather than putting two of the Devil's Own completely out of commission.

Then, suddenly, his gaze flicked beyond her toward the parking garage. His expression darkened perceptibly.

Oh, God! What now? The rest of the Devil's Own? Laura wondered, looking frantically in the same direction only to see that the big silver Cadillac and the little red Toyota they'd been watching so diligently all night were nowhere in sight. The elderly Lothario and his young tootsie had apparently escaped unseen, not to mention unphotographed by that stalwart shamus, Zachary, S. U.

"Great. That's just great." While Sam growled, he held out his hand for Laura's and pulled her to her feet.

It was only then, when she stood up, that she realized she was shaking, wobbling pitifully in her tar-stained high heels. "Wh...what do we do now?" she asked.

Sam had reached down for the blanket and was

snapping it smartly into a small square. "Now," he said, "we haul these two clowns down six flights of stairs and deliver them to the guys at the Fourth Precinct."

He handed her the folded blanket, and when she took it with her trembling hands, Sam didn't let go immediately. "It's okay," he said softly, his eyes warm in the moonlight and steady on hers. "It's all right now, Laura. It's all over. Nobody's going to hurt you."

All she could do was work up a weak, wobbly smile. "Thanks."

Sam smiled. "Hey, you hired me to protect you, right? I'm just doing my job." He angled his head toward the parking lot, then added glumly, "Well, one of them, anyway. It looks like we're all through here, so after we get rid of these jerks, we'll go get that tall, cold drink I promised you."

Laura managed a feeble, grateful nod. "C-could you make it Scotch? A d-double?"

The Ten-Gallon Hat, on Highway Z, was a hole-in-the-wall that billed itself as a roadhouse. By day it looked more like a one-story cement block warehouse, but by night its miles of neon tubing made it look bigger and brighter and a lot more fun than any place else in the county. Sam had spent a lot of time here after Jenny's accident, but he didn't remember having any fun.

It was two-fifteen in the morning but the band was still playing when Sam ushered Laura across a floor strewn with peanut shells and discarded beer caps to a small booth in the back, where he hoped her outfit wouldn't attract too much attention. At least not the sort that would require further use of his bruised knuckles.

Lynette, one of the two overworked waitresses in the place, took their order without her usual chitchat, but she still managed to give Sam a few meaningful looks and whisper, "It's nice to see you with a date, hon."

"She's not a date," Sam responded gruffly.

"Coulda fooled me," Lynette whispered back before she disappeared into the crowd on the dance floor.

Then, after their drinks came, along with more meaningful looks, they sat quietly awhile. Laura played with the swizzle stick in her double Scotch and water, while Sam rolled his cold beer bottle across the back of one hand and then the other, trying not to wince.

It had been the first time in his dubious career as a private investigator that he'd had to use his fists. Part of him was glad to know he hadn't lost much speed, but the rest of him—his aching knuckles, mostly—was protesting vehemently.

"Thank you, Sam." Laura's voice floated over the music and across the scarred tabletop. "For defending me."

"No big deal. I told you. It's what you're paying me for." He took a long pull from the beer bottle. "Anyway, it was pretty stupid of me to take you to that part of town and put you in harm's way like that. I guess I wasn't thinking. Probably just too used to working alone."

Too used to *being* alone, he added to himself.

"Well, I don't suppose these clothes helped any, either." Her gaze fluttered downward for a moment.

"I can only guess what kind of babe good old Jerome and Swat thought they'd discovered up there on the roof." She gave a tiny shrug then. "Will they go to jail?"

"If I press charges," Sam said.

Her eyes widened. "If?"

"I'm going to assume they learned a pretty good lesson tonight."

"Sure." Laura snorted. "They probably learned that they ought to use guns next time instead of knives." She sipped her drink, then said, "And speaking of learning, where did you learn to throw a punch like that?"

"I did some boxing in college, then later in the Marine Corps."

"I'm impressed."

"Don't be," he told her. "I wasn't all that good." He touched a finger to his nose, where an unexpected left hook had left a small, but permanent detour in the cartilage. "This used to be a lot straighter."

Even though she'd barely made a dent in her Scotch, her smile already had a slightly inebriated tilt to it. It went well with the blue velvet dress, Sam decided. She went well with the blue velvet dress.

"I have a confession to make, Zachary S. U." she said as she traced the rim of her glass with a fingertip.

"What's that?"

"I thought I had made a big mistake about hiring you. I was even thinking, earlier tonight, about asking you for a refund, and hiring somebody different. Somebody, um, well…better."

He raised an eyebrow. "And?"

"I know now I didn't make a mistake." She

leaned her head back against the booth's battered wooden frame, then let out a long sigh as she closed her eyes. "I feel safe with you."

She wouldn't have, Sam thought, if she knew the direction in which his mind was tending while his gaze roamed unhindered over her relaxed face and figure. About all that separated him from Jerome and Swat right that moment was a willingness to obey the law. That and the fact that they were in a public place. Otherwise...

Otherwise what, for God's sake?

He jerked upright and squared his shoulders, then downed the last of his beer and put the bottle down with a solid thump, loud enough to cause Laura's eyes to pop open.

"It's time to go," he said, already sliding out of the booth. "Come on."

Sleep wouldn't come that night. Not even after the three fingers of Jack Daniel's Black that Sam had poured as a last resort. Instead of putting him to sleep, all the bourbon did was give him a headache. And it failed miserably in blunting his desire for the woman who slept in the room across the hall.

For the hundredth time he checked the glowing blue numbers on the clock radio, realizing it would be dawn in less than half an hour. Pretty soon he'd be able to distinguish the muted plaid pattern of the wallpaper, the spiderweb fracture of the windowpane where he'd connected on one of Davey Kenyon's curveballs in eighth grade, the dozens of trophies on the desktop and bookshelves that could use a good dusting.

He didn't even need daylight to see the objects in

this room where he'd spent most of his nights for most of his life. Most of all he didn't need light of any sort to see Jenny's face smiling out at him from the silver-framed photograph on top of the knotty pine dresser. It was always there, that mischievous, gamine face that he'd loved from the very first day of kindergarten when he'd come home—right here— and announced to his mother over cookies and milk that he was going to marry Jenny Sayles, then asked in all seriousness just how long he'd have to wait to do that.

Although his mother had laughed and suggested a seemly eighteen or twenty years might be good, her answer should have been forever.

Sam felt that too-familiar constriction in his throat now and the hot sheen of moisture in his eyes that always came when he allowed himself to think about Jenny for more than a passing moment. Swearing softly, he reached up to double the pillow under his head, then he closed his eyes, for all the good that would do in blocking out nearly three decades of images that seemed almost permanently etched on his brain. Jenny here. Jenny there. Jenny everywhere.

Since he couldn't marry her in kindergarten, he'd waited until their graduation from high school to ask her. She'd put him off, and then put him off again when they graduated from college. It wasn't that she didn't want to marry him. She did. She swore she did. But Jenny had her own itinerary. She wanted to go as far as she could as a concert pianist before settling in as Sam's wife. And she thought she had all the time in the world. They both did.

His gaze lit on the Divisional boxing trophy he'd won in the Corps. When Jenny moved to Los Angeles to study with the renowned pianist, Hermoine Stahl, it made perfect sense for Sam to enlist in the Marine Corps because Camp Pendleton was just a few hours away from L.A. Later, when Jenny moved to Paris, he pulled a string or two in order to be assigned embassy duty there. Wherever Jenny went, he followed. It had been *whither thou goest* in reverse.

When Jenny acquired a rampant case of stage fright that prevented her from performing, he'd resigned from the Corps and followed her back here where he'd run for county sheriff, winning in a surprising landslide. But even then, Jenny wouldn't marry him. She needed to prove she could play on stage, if only one more time.

And then, on an icy stretch of Highway A-14, Jenny's time had run out.

It was light enough now for Sam's eyes to trace all the hairline cracks in the ceiling. He wondered how many men his age had only loved one woman in their lives, and of those how many had only made love to one woman. Damned few, he decided.

While Jenny was alive, he'd been oblivious to other women. In the two years since her death, he'd been both oblivious and numb. Then suddenly Laura McNeal had waltzed out of the Yellow Pages and into his office in her little blue velvet scrap of a dress, and had lit a fire in him that Sam didn't like one bit.

He sat up now, rubbing nonexistent sleep out of his eyes. He should've known better than to offer to help the woman. But, since he had, he was going to help her with a vengeance. Help her right out of his life.

Chapter 4

The next morning, for lack of a garbage truck to grind and groan outside her window at the crack of dawn, Laura didn't wake up until nine-thirty. There was a note taped to the bathroom mirror. *Back soon. Make yourself at home.*

Then, once again in her pathetic search for something to wear, Laura wandered across the hall to stand in the center of the faded, circular rag rug in Sam's bedroom, looking around, shaking her head in dismay and disbelief. And people called *her* weird for clinging to the past, she thought.

Being in Sam's room, with its maple bunk bed and boyish plaid wallpaper and sturdy hopsacking café curtains, was like time traveling back two or three, maybe even four, decades. It was a bit like suddenly finding herself smack in the middle of an episode of *Leave It to Beaver.*

There were felt pennants tacked here and there on

the wall, all of them thickly furred with dust. The bookshelves were dusty, too, and crammed with old textbooks and chunky 8-track tapes and ancient, faded copies of *National Geographic*. She inspected the desktop with its assortment of trophies, half expecting to find a prom ticket and an assignment notebook hidden among them. Boxing. Baseball. Football. Hmm.

And who, pray tell, was this waif-like brunette in the sterling silver frame? Laura ran a finger across the top of the frame, finding it to be just about the only dustless surface in the room.

Very interesting. *Very* interesting. Sam, you devil, you.

It wasn't that she was snooping, exactly, even though she was incredibly curious about Zachary, S. U., especially after he'd decked those two thugs, Jerome and Swat, last night without even blinking or breaking a sweat. The guy had turned into Superman right before her very eyes on that rooftop. Bam! Blam! Then, just as quickly, he'd reverted to his quiet, self-effacing alter ego, Clark Kent.

If Clark Kent had a bedroom, Laura thought now, this is exactly the way it would look.

Well, maybe she *was* snooping a little, she admitted to herself, but it was just an honest by-product of trying to find something to wear. Having awakened in her bra and panties, she'd taken one look at the blue velvet dress and decided she couldn't bear to put it on again. Not just because it was pretty bizarre out here in West Overshoes, but also because it was merchandise intended for the shop and she didn't want to wear it out. Bad enough she'd have to pay to have it dry-cleaned now before she put it on the rack at Nana's Attic.

Having already rejected Sam's mother's clothes because of their fragrance, she was hoping to find a T-shirt and perhaps a pair of pants with a drawstring to adjust them from Sam's size to her own.

Then, instead of searching for something to wear, she'd been distracted by this time warped room and its ancient contents. With the exception of one or two current news magazines and paperbacks, it looked as if nothing had changed here since the seventies. Certainly nothing had been dusted in months and months. Well, except for Lois Lane over there in her shiny silver frame.

She was going to take a much closer look at the photograph when a car door slammed in the driveway. All of a sudden Laura felt horribly furtive, like a thief in the night, or worse, like a snoopy woman poking around where it was none of her business. A half-naked snoop at that, she thought, glimpsing herself in the oval mirror above the knotty pine dresser.

Deciding it was too late to find a top *and* a bottom, Laura opened the closet and yanked a blue oxford cloth shirt off a hanger. The cuffs cascaded past her fingertips and the shirttails hit her at the knees, but at least she was decently covered, she thought, as she trotted down the stairs to greet Sam.

The key was already scritching in the lock on the back door when Laura entered the kitchen. The knob rattled to no avail, then the key scritched and scraped again. Sam, it seemed, was back in full Clark Kent mode, unable to even get in his own back door. For some silly reason, that made Laura smile.

"Wait a minute, Sam," she called, rolling up the

too-long sleeves on her way to throw the stubborn
bolt and open the door for him. "There. I hope you
don't mind the shirt. I..."

It wasn't Sam.

It was a woman who looked just as astonished to
see Laura as Laura was to see her. The woman
blinked as she jerked the key out of the lock, and for
a second her mouth moved, but no words came out.
Then she stuttered, "I...I'm so sorry. I had no idea
that Sam..."

Her gaze skittered down the front of the big shirt,
to Laura's bare feet, and then back to her face. "I...I
didn't know Sam had...that he...that he was seeing
someone."

"Seeing?"

It took a second for the woman's meaning to register, and when it did, Laura started to laugh, thinking
she probably did look like she had just slipped out
of Sam's bed and into his shirt. "It's really not what
it looks like. Believe me. I'm just a client."

The woman had stopped blinking. Now she just
stared, pretty suspiciously, too, in Laura's opinion.
She was wearing a sleeveless cotton dress, Laura
noted, and more than an everyday application of
makeup. Lipstick, eyeshadow, liner, mascara, blush.
The whole nine yards. Not a single brunette hair was
out of place on the woman's head, either. Somehow
she looked vaguely familiar, and then it suddenly occurred to Laura that this was none other than Lois
Lane, the face in the dustless silver frame upstairs in
Sam's room.

Uh-oh.

"You're Sam's client?" Lois asked now, although

it was really more of a nasty accusation than a question.

"Yes, his client," Laura insisted. "I hired Sam to…well…he's sort of my bodyguard." Not that it's any of your business, Lois, honey, she added to herself. She might have even said it out loud except just that moment Sam's big Chevy Blazer crunched into the driveway and rolled to a stop.

"Oh, there's Sam." Lois was suddenly all smiles. "Well, good luck with your problem," she called over her shoulder as she made a beeline for the Blazer, or more precisely for its driver.

Great Caesar's ghost. Laura sighed and leaned a shoulder against the doorjamb, while she watched Sam's big, goofy smile as he greeted the woman. If she'd gotten the poor man in a world of trouble, she'd make it up to him somehow. Still, the way the little brunette was standing close to him, reaching out to touch his arm or his hand or his cheek, smiling up into his face, it appeared as if all had been forgiven already.

Good, Laura thought, even as she was aware of a tiny tic of disappointment somewhere deep inside her which didn't make any sense at all. Sam Zachary wasn't hers to lose. Not only that, he wasn't her type. She was a city mouse, born and bred, and not the least inclined to country bumpkins. And over and above all that, she reminded herself, she'd sworn off men completely. Who needed them? All they ever did was leave.

She was standing at the sink, downing a tall glass of cool water, her back to the door, when he came in.

"Good morning," he said.

"Good morning." Laura turned to find him giving her a slow and thorough once-over from head to toe.

"Nice outfit," he said.

How she could have forgotten she was wearing his shirt, Laura didn't know, but now she squinched herself smaller and shorter to make sure the shirttails covered everything. "I hope you don't mind," she said.

He shook his head. "No, I don't mind. It looks a lot better on you than on me."

For a second she swore he was blushing like some big, dopey teenager, the one who slept in the time machine upstairs, then his expression cooled.

"Here," he said, offering her a paper grocery bag. "I stopped in town and picked up a few things just to tide you over."

Laura took the bag, peeked in to see jeans, a T-shirt or two, a pair of sneakers, a hairbrush and toothbrush and some pastel underthings. Her underthings! She'd bought the matching pink lace bra and panties only three or four weeks ago. "These are mine," she exclaimed.

"Well...yeah."

"But where did you get them?"

His mouth stayed closed, but his eyes widened and his whole face seemed to say *Well, duh.* "At your place," he finally said. "Where else?"

"How did you know where I lived?" The subject hadn't come up. Laura was certain of that. "I never told you where I lived."

"You didn't?" He scratched his head, shrugged, then grinned. "I must be one hell of a detective, then. I left some frozen stuff in the car. Be right back."

* * *

An hour later, Laura was putting down her fork on her plate and letting out a long, satisfied sigh. "I don't know about your detecting skills, but you're one hell of a cook, Sam. What did you put in that omelette?"

"Fennel." He was sifting a second spoonful of sugar into his coffee as he spoke. "Did you like it?"

Laura nodded even though she didn't have a clue what fennel was. Probably something else from his locust-plagued garden. A little shiver raced down her spine at the mere thought.

"Thanks for getting my clothes," she said, watching in mute horror as he dipped back into the sugar bowl for a third heaping teaspoon, wondering why he didn't weigh a thousand pounds.

As it turned out, Sam had remembered the name of her shop—Nana's Attic—and had gone there first thing this morning to retrieve some clothes for her. Brian, her part-time assistant, had directed Sam to the apartment upstairs.

"You're welcome," he said, stirring his treacly brew.

"Thank you, too, for not telling Brian where I am or what happened. It would just upset him."

"No problem. Did I tell you he said not to worry, that he could keep the place open until you came back?"

"Yes, you did, but I don't mind hearing it again. I need as much business as I can get since I can barely pay the rent as it is."

"Not much demand for secondhand clothes, huh?"

"Vintage clothes," she corrected him, glaring a little over the rim of her own cup of pure, unadorned, undiluted black coffee, then inquiring irritably, "If you don't like coffee, Sam, why in the world do you drink it?"

"You mean the sugar?" He looked guiltily at his cup. "It's just a habit, I guess. Beats smoking."

"Well, it's a bad one, nevertheless." Laura picked up their plates and carried them to the sink. "I'll do these," she said. "You probably have to get back to work."

When he didn't answer, she looked over her shoulder. "You do have to get back to work, don't you?"

He shook his head. "I am working," he said.

"Oh."

Laura felt another inexplicable little stitch of disappointment inside her. Of course, he was working. He was working for her. She knew that. This wasn't a date, for heaven's sake, or even two pals getting together over brunch. Theirs was a purely professional relationship.

She turned the water on to rinse the plates, raised her voice over its noise. "I met your lady friend. She seems nice."

"My what?" He was standing so close behind her that Laura jumped.

"Your lady friend. The woman who was here when you got home."

Sam was reaching around her, running a coffee cup under the hot stream of water. "Janey?" He chuckled. "She's not my lady friend. What made you think that?"

"I don't know. She seemed…well…possessive of you, not all that thrilled to see me here." Pretty ticked, actually, although Laura didn't add that.

"Well, we've known each other a long time. Forever. I guess maybe Janey does tend to be a little possessive. I was engaged to her older sister, Jenny.''

''Was?''

He dumped the sugary dregs of his coffee into the sink. ''She died,'' he said.

''Oh, Sam.'' Laura whirled around and found herself practically in his embrace. ''How awful for you. I'm so sorry.''

''It's okay.'' He didn't step back when she turned, but stood there, slightly off balance, one hand still reaching into the sink, the other now coming forward to brace himself on the edge of the counter.

If there was even an inch between them, Laura couldn't tell because the space seemed to be filled with tangible heat. Sam's warm brown eyes flickered with desire while an odd smile—part wistful, part wanting—cut across his lips. It made Laura's heart free-fall to the pit of her stomach.

Then suddenly he shifted his weight, stepping back, removing his arms from that almost-but-not-quite embrace. ''It's okay,'' he said again. ''It happened a long time ago.''

''Even so...''

''Thanks for doing the dishes,'' he said, cutting her off not only with words but with a resumption of a neutral expression. It was as if he'd donned a mask. ''I've got some work to do in my office downstairs. It shouldn't take too long. Just make yourself comfortable, okay?''

''Sure. Okay.''

He walked to a door just off of the kitchen, but to Laura, Sam Zachary looked like a man who would have broken into an open-field run if only he had had the distance.

* * *

It had been a long time since Sam had felt the stirrings of desire. In the two years since Jenny's death, he really hadn't even looked at a woman until Miss Laura McNeal came through his office door, planted herself in the chair across from his, and then somehow—probably through his own damned misguided gallantry—planted herself in his life. Like a weed, he thought. A ditzy little dandelion. No. Worse. Like pernicious Velvet Leaf.

This morning he had stood in the bedroom of her apartment, gazing at the jumble of sky blue sheets and blue-and-yellow patchwork quilts on her unmade bed, feeling more than a little like a Peeping Tom, fighting the urge to press a rumpled pillowcase to his nose in search of Laura's fragrance.

When he'd opened a bureau drawer in search of clothes, his fingers had drifted longer than they should have through the tumbled silks and laces. Just now, upstairs in the kitchen, when she'd turned and they'd stood so close...

He didn't need this. He'd almost kissed her. He must be nuts.

Sam wrenched off his polo shirt and jeans, then stabbed his legs and arms into his worn gray sweats. He lowered himself onto the seat of his rowing machine, intent on working out ferociously until his mind was a total blank and his body gave up desire in favor of pain.

He was rowing across the Atlantic.

He'd begun the punishing trip a week after Jenny's funeral and one day after he'd resigned his job as county sheriff. It was either that or choosing between the slow death of bourbon versus the quick oblivion of his service revolver.

So Sam rowed.

In his imagination, he began his journey at the southern tip of Staten Island, hugging the fortieth parallel, his back to the east, his destination a deserted beach in Portugal that was, by his calculations, three thousand eight hundred seventy-two miles away. In two years and two months, at a steady pace of four miles an hour, across an ocean smooth as glass, he ought to have been only seven hundred miles shy of that Portugese beach today.

But there was always weather, which depended on his mood, and since his moods were stormy more often than not, full of squalls and sou'westers and occasional raging tempests, as of today he had traveled exactly fifteen hundred eighty-one miles, putting him dead in the middle of the North Atlantic.

Right now it was blowing up a storm. Hurricane Laura.

Sam used every muscle in his body, every ounce of strength he had to pull against the hard currents and high waves and punishing winds. An hour later, his gray sweats were dark and heavy with perspiration, and rather than four miles ahead, he marked his course at eight miles back at fifteen hundred seventy-three.

Laura was dusting in the living room when he came upstairs to take a shower. Where she'd found the red-feathered duster was a mystery to Sam. Why she was humming so cheerfully was even more of a mystery. A woman on the run from a lover who'd punched her in the eye and threatened further violence shouldn't be so damned chipper. But at least she wasn't wearing that skimpy blue outfit anymore, he thought at the same instant that he noticed the snug fit of the seat of her jeans and the firm curves outlined by her T-shirt.

"You don't have to do that," he said from the foot of the stairs.

"I know," she called back, standing on tiptoe and stretching to reach the curtain tops. "I just wanted to keep busy."

That was what he should do, Sam decided. Keep busy. Start thinking with his brain instead of the area considerably south of his head. It had been a mistake, bringing Laura here for safekeeping, but he'd just have to deal with it until he could come up with a better plan.

He started up the stairs, but stopped when Laura called out, "The phone rang while you were in the basement, Sam. I didn't think you heard it, so I answered, but whoever was on the other end of the line hung up without saying anything."

"Okay. Thanks," he said. "I've got Caller ID on the extension upstairs. I'll check it out."

Sam took a last glance over his shoulder at the woman happily flitting red feathers across all the junk in his living room, then trotted up the stairs. There was only one call registered on the ID screen, and he recognized it immediately. Janey Sayles. He sighed out loud.

He'd known Jenny's younger sister almost all of his life. Janey might as well have been his own sister. He'd tried hard to be there for her, to be a dependable big brother, even before Jenny's accident. Years ago, when Janey asked him to take her to her junior and senior proms, he'd been happy to oblige. He'd attended her high school graduation, helped her move into her dorm at college, helped her move out when she was homesick three weeks later.

When Janey came to visit Jenny in California, it had been Sam who'd played escort at Disneyland and Knott's Berry Farm. In Paris, too, when she'd come to visit Jenny there. In fact, the only request of Janey's he'd ever refused was to be her Lamaze coach three years ago when she gave birth to her out-of-wedlock child.

"Why doesn't she ask you?" he'd asked Jenny, who'd laughed and replied, "Because she's not in love with *me,* silly."

Sam hadn't believed it then, and he didn't believe it now. Janey Sayles was just lonely, even more so after Jenny's death. Hell, *he* was lonely. He punched her numbers into the phone, and after a long series of rings, he heard her muted hello.

"It's Sam, Janey."

She didn't sound surprised, but then he always returned her calls as quickly as he could. She had called, Janey told him, to cancel the roast chicken dinner she had promised to fix him that evening. As soon as she said it, Sam realized he'd forgotten all about it. He put another mental black mark in Laura McNeal's column.

"No problem," he said. "We'll do it some other time."

"Sure. Okay." Janey sounded distracted. "The reason I need to cancel dinner is because Samantha's not feeling too well. She's running a temperature and her eyes look kind of glassy."

"Poor baby." Sam meant it. His three-year-old

goddaughter, Samantha, was one of the few bright spots in his life these days. Still, Janey had a tendency to overreact even to a sniffle. "Give her a hug for me, will you?"

"Sure." Janey was so quiet then that Sam almost thought she'd hung up until she said softly, "Sam?"

"What?"

"How long is that…that person going to be there?"

It took a second for her question to register. "Laura, you mean?"

"Oh. Is that her name? She claimed to be one of your clients."

"Yeah. She is. She's on the run from an overly aggressive boyfriend. I couldn't think of any place else to stash her."

"I see. So she won't be staying there too long, then?"

"Not if I can help it," Sam said.

"Well, I'd better go take Samantha's temperature again. Maybe we can do that dinner next week. Bye, Sam."

She hung up so abruptly that Sam didn't have time to say goodbye, much less ask if there was anything he could do for Samantha. He was debating driving the four miles to Janey's place when he heard a crash downstairs.

Laura pulled a footstool over to the fireplace and stood atop it in order to dust the mirror over the mantel. The big mirror had probably been hanging there for decades relatively undisturbed, but the instant she touched it with the feather duster, it fell.

The damned thing took out every knickknack on

the mantelpiece before it crashed to the floor. And Laura, wobbling precariously on the three-legged footstool, wasn't far behind. She landed hard in a field of broken glass.

Mirror glass and Venetian glass and art glass.

Carnival glass.

Depression glass.

Man, wasn't that the truth!

With the breath knocked out of her, Laura just sat there. She picked up a cup handle, pondered it dismally while she heard Sam come barreling down the stairs. A second later, he cannonballed into the living room, pointing a gun at her.

"Go ahead. Shoot me," she said mournfully. "I deserve it."

"What the hell were you doing?" he asked, setting the pistol on a table and advancing toward her across the smithereens. "Are you all right?"

Laura nodded. "I was just dusting. It doesn't seem to be my forte. I'm so sorry about all..." She gestured wanly to the broken glass that surrounded her. "...this."

In a effort to get up, she braced her hand on the floor only to get a sliver of glass stuck painfully in her palm. "Ouch. Dammit."

"Don't move," Sam ordered as he crunched across the shards.

He towered over her a moment—a colossus—his legs in the gray sweats looking like two cement highway supports. Then, the next thing Laura knew, he had swept her up in his arms.

"I'm so sorry, Sam." She tilted her head against his damp sweatshirt. "I know how much all this old stuff means to you, how attached you are to it."

"I'm not attached to it." He crunched more glass underfoot as he carried her into the hallway. "It's just here. That's all," he grumbled. "And I'm here."

So you are, Sam Zachary, Laura thought as he stood there holding her as if he never meant to let her go.

So you are. And so, it seemed, was she. For the time being, at least.

She told herself to treasure the moment, wallow in it even, because in her experience, men always meant to let her go.

Well, except for rotten Artie.

Chapter 5

Sam spent the rest of the day working on his garden
out in back of the house where the little city slicker
was loathe to go. He had planned to use the rototiller
to break up another forty or fifty square feet of
ground, but after holding Laura's lush body in his
arms, he figured a couple hours of hard labor was
what he needed to banish the feel of her from his
senses and the thought of her from his brain.

Even after the clouds moved in and the rain began
to splatter down, he continued to drive the spade
deep into the earth, turning over the clay soil, adding
mulch, and working it all into a soft, friable loam.
Every once in a while he'd hear the sound of broken
glass tinkling into the trash can just outside the back
door, but not once did he look in that direction. Well,
once. Okay, maybe twice. But never for more than
ten or fifteen seconds.

He felt so damned disloyal. Like one of the straying husbands in his case files. He'd spent the past two years in an emotional and physical limbo, and now, a mere twenty-four hours after Laura walked into his office, that limbo had turned to lust. He was ashamed of the heat that he couldn't cool off, no matter what he did, and the need that he couldn't deny.

When the rain increased from soft patter to outright pouring, he took his tools to the shed then went back into the house, eventually discovering Laura curled up on the front porch swing.

"Nice rain," she said softly.

"We need it." Sam angled a hip onto the wooden railing. If they remained six feet apart as they were at the moment and only discussed the weather, he figured he could handle it.

She stretched her arms over her head, which caused her T-shirt to pull out of her jeans, revealing a few inches of sleek midriff.

"Are you hungry?" she asked.

Oh, yeah. Sam's gaze jerked back to her face. "Famished."

"Let's call out for a pizza. My treat."

He laughed. "Do you have any idea how close the nearest pizza place is?" When she shook her head, he gestured over his shoulder and said, "About seventeen miles as the crow flies."

"Oh." It was her turn to laugh. "Sorry. I keep forgetting I'm out here in West Overshoes," she said, riffling her fingers through her blond hair as she gave the swing a push.

"Southwest Overshoes, technically," he said.

"Sorry."

There was a low roll of thunder in the distance.

Laura shivered and appeared to sink farther into the cushions, as if making herself a smaller target, and once again Sam found himself wrestling with the urge to wrap his arms around her. Dammit. He wished he'd stop doing that. He needed to get his mind on something else. Abruptly, he levered off the porch rail.

"What do you like on your pizza?" he asked.

"Excuse me?"

"I said I'll fix us a pizza. What do you like on it?"

"Oh." She blinked. "You mean fix a pizza from scratch?"

"Yep. What do you like?"

"Well, anchovies and black olives, actually."

Sam sighed. Why the hell had he asked? "How about sausage, green pepper, and onions?"

"Sure. That'd be fine, too. What can I do to help?"

"Just drape yourself over a chair, sip a little wine and keep me company," he said.

She laughed. "I can do that."

"Yeah. I was pretty sure you could."

While Laura thought it was kind of cute to make a pizza from scratch, she thought that pureeing homegrown tomatoes to make the sauce that had to simmer for nearly an hour was going a bit overboard. Way overboard, in fact. Hadn't he ever heard of Prego sauce? she wondered.

As ordered, she sat in the kitchen, sipping her wine and keeping him company. But by the time Sam dipped his wooden spoon into the pot, tasted the sauce and deemed it "just right," Laura was half blitzed.

Not only that, but the storm was getting worse. The wind seemed to be really picking up and thunder was rattling the windowpanes. She hated storms. They terrified her. They always had.

When she was little, her father used to wrap his big warm arms around her for protection, and sing funny songs that made her forget about the storm. Then, after he disappeared, Laura took to hiding in a cobwebby corner of Nana's attic, pretending she was as small as a mouse, if not invisible. Her mother and Nana kept telling her that she shouldn't be so afraid, that the house was grounded, but she didn't know what that meant or how it could keep her safe the way her daddy's arms once had.

Now a nearby snap of lightning and simultaneous thunder almost brought her out of her chair.

"It's okay," Sam said, glancing over his shoulder from his stalwart post at the stove. "The house is grounded."

"Oh, good." She still didn't know what that meant or why it ought to make her feel any less afraid.

Laura poured a little more liquid courage in her glass, then went to the freezer for a few ice cubes, hating to water down the good red wine, but knowing that by the time the pizza was done, she would be, too, if she didn't take a few precautionary measures.

She leaned against the refrigerator a moment, trying to look as casual and unconcerned as Sam, then reminded herself this was a huge electrical appliance, probably capable of delivering a gazillion watts right into her hundred fifteen pound, highly conductive frame, so she returned to her chair at the table.

Another bolt of lightning hit. The lights flickered.

"Mind if I wander down to the basement?" she asked, her hand already on the knob.

By the time Sam replied, "No. I don't mind. Go ahead," she had flipped the wall switch and was halfway down the stairs.

Like most basements, this one was half creepy and half comfortably inhabited. Laura turned right toward the paneled room with its antiquated red-and-green checkerboard tile floor. She wasn't surprised by the big recliner chair or the rowing machine or the treadmill. The piano, however, was rather unexpected. It was a beautiful, old mahogany spinet with delicately carved legs.

On closer inspection, she could see that there wasn't a speck of dust on it. The lesson book propped on the music stand was open, its pages full of red penciled notations, some dated as recently as this week. Laura closed the book enough to read the title. *You're Never Too Old—Teach Yourself Piano in Twenty EZ Lessons.*

"Oh, Sam," she murmured softly. Her Superman P.I. wasn't just a gourmet cook and a master gardener. He played the piano, too. She smiled now, suspecting that stashed away somewhere in the house was a needlepoint pillow in progress or a macrame plant holder Sam worked on in the dead of night.

Overhead, she heard the muted crash of thunder. The lights flickered again. Then they went out. Laura was swamped in darkness.

"Sam!"

He didn't answer.

"Sam!" she called again, to no avail.

Okay, don't panic, she told herself. It's just dark. That's all. It was so dark she didn't dare move for fear of tripping over the rowing machine or breaking her neck on the treadmill.

"Sam!"

No answer.

Laura swallowed hard, but it didn't do a thing to dislodge the panic that was closing her throat, preventing her from calling out again. There was only one thing she could think of to do.

She felt her way to the piano bench, sat, found middle C, and proceeded to bang out her own version of an SOS—the world's loudest, and probably worst, rendition of "Chopsticks."

Sam ducked his head and came sideways down the narrow stairs, following the beam of his flashlight.

When the electricity had cut out, he'd been upstairs searching for candles, telling himself repeatedly that he was taking wise precautions in a storm rather than trying to do something as hopelessly romantic as a candlelight dinner. In the sudden dark, the first thing he'd done was offer silent thanks for the gas stove where the pizza was baking. Then the silence was broken by the bashing of piano keys in the basement.

She was still bashing them as he made his way down the dark stairs.

"You can stop now," he yelled.

When she didn't, he aimed the light right at her and yelled again, "Laura, it's okay. You can stop now."

She turned in the light, her blue eyes dilated and

wide with fear. "I called and I called, Sam. I didn't know where you were."

"I'm right here." He sat next to her on the bench, nudging her over a few inches with his hip. He put the flashlight atop the piano, its beam angled away from them into a far corner of the room.

Laura tilted her head against his shoulder and slid her arms around his waist. "I'm such a wimp," she said, "but storms just terrify me."

"It's okay. You're safe," he said, suddenly questioning his own safety, as well as his ability to batten down his increasing, improbable desire for this woman. Not knowing what to do with his hands, Sam placed them on the keyboard. Then, feeling like a total jerk, he began playing the last piece he had committed to memory. Liszt's "Liebestraum."

The sweet, dreamy chords drowned out the rumbling sound of thunder overhead.

"That's beautiful," Laura said on a long sigh, her head still on his shoulder, her arms still clamped around him.

Sam knew it wasn't. He was grateful Laura didn't seem to pick up on the tremor in his fingers or notice his amateurish hesitation in three-quarter time. If they'd been dancing, he thought, this was the equivalent of stepping all over her feet.

"It sounds like a lullaby," she whispered. "What is it?"

"Liebestraum," he said, still playing. "A dream of love."

An *EZ* piece, he thought disgustedly. The watered-down beginner's version of the waltz his Jenny used to play so perfectly, so effortlessly. Ah, God. What was he doing, wanting somebody else?

"Mmm. It's a lovely dream. You're good, Sam."

"No, I'm not," he said, coming more or less to his senses while he stabbed out a crude "Shave and a Haircut," and sat up straighter in order to shrug off Laura's lolling head and disengage her arms.

He reached for the flashlight. "Come on. The pizza should be almost finished by now."

"This is fabulous," Laura said, licking her fingers while she eyed the untouched piece on Sam's plate, where he had just conclusively tucked his napkin. "Aren't you going to eat that?"

"Go for it," he said, pushing the plate her way.

Laura reached between the two candles burning in the center of the kitchen table and snatched up her fifth piece of what had to be the world's greatest pizza. The crust was to die for, and the sauce! All the fussing and that interminable hour of simmering had definitely paid off.

"You should start a franchise, Sam," she said, plopping an errant strand of mozzarella back onto the slice.

His response was a fairly wan smile that hardly crinkled his eyes at all. In fact, he'd been pretty subdued, almost distant, ever since coming up from the basement. He probably considered her a total wimp for the way she behaved in the storm. Lois Lane, no doubt, ate lightning and thunder for breakfast.

But his distance had a sadness in it, too, and Laura suspected it had something to do with the song he had played on the piano, but when she'd asked him if it brought back memories, he made it pretty clear that, even if it did, he didn't want to discuss them. Not with her, anyway.

She kept having to remind herself that theirs wasn't a personal relationship. It was purely professional. She had hired Zachary, S. U. to keep her safe from Artie Hammerman. He wasn't some gigolo, after all, whom she'd retained to wine and dine her, to get her all hot and bothered.

Artie! Laura realized all of a sudden that she hadn't thought about him in hours. She even kept forgetting that her eye was now a stunning combination of purple and black and blue, and soon it would be turning a spectacular and queasy greenish-yellow. Little wonder Sam didn't find her all that attractive. Even in the candlelight, she must've looked like a featherweight who'd lost a recent bout. Well, she supposed she had.

With her appetite suddenly gone, she put the last bit of pizza back on her plate. The storm had slackened to simple rain. She wasn't terrified anymore. Maybe it was time to be brave. About everything. About everyone.

"I probably ought to be coming up with some sort of plan for dealing with Artie," she said. "I don't want to take advantage of your hospitality or overstay my welcome. Plus, to tell you the truth, Sam, I can't afford you all that much longer. What was it you quoted me? A hundred dollars a day?"

"We'll talk about it tomorrow," he said. A little grin tipped up the corners of his mouth. "Never decide anything by candlelight, Laura. That's my motto. You'll always regret it."

As if on cue, the lights came back on and the refrigerator resumed its low, reassuring hum. Both Laura and Sam laughed softly. Sam cupped his hand around a flame and blew out one candle, then the other.

"We'll come up with some kind of a plan tomorrow," he said. "I'll clean up the kitchen. Why don't you just go on to bed."

From his tone, Laura got the distinct impression that Sam wasn't just being polite. He wanted to be alone. She wasn't the least bit sleepy, but she faked a yawn just to make him feel better.

"Good night, Sam. See you in the morning."

"See you in the morning," he echoed, sounding not at all enthusiastic about the prospect.

He saw her well before morning.

In fact, just a little after midnight, another storm front rolled through, nearly as violent as its predecessor. Sam hadn't been able to fall asleep, so he lay in his bottom bunk listening to the wind as it lashed the branches of the pines and pin oaks that surrounded the house, worrying about the gazing ball in the sideyard but not enough to rush outside to retrieve it, hoping Laura was sound asleep and unaware of the fierce lightning and thunder.

Once or twice, he considered going across the hall and checking on her, but rejected the idea each time it occurred. No sense tempting fate. No sense tempting *himself*. He was a one-woman man. The fact that his woman was dead hadn't changed that.

Most of him was dead, too. He was just going through the motions now. The gardening, the cooking, the rowing, the piano—they were just preoccupations to keep him sane. His occupation, the P.I. business, was nothing more than a way of paying the bills.

A close bolt of lightning colored his room blue for a moment and lit up Jenny's face in its silver frame on his desk. Sam's throat closed. He felt so alone that even Jenny looked like a stranger.

Shifting onto his side, Sam glanced at the glowing digits on his clock radio at the exact moment they winked out and thunder shook the house right down to the foundation.

"Sam?" Laura's frightened voice sounded close by his bed. She must've covered the distance between their rooms in record time. "May I sleep in here? Just for a little while?"

"Sure." He threw back the covers and slung his legs to the floor. "The top bunk's all made up, but there's no ladder. Here. I'll give you a hand up."

He reached out his hand for hers in the dark. It wasn't her hand he made contact with, but rather the warm curve of her waist, covered by thin cotton, unencumbered by any sort of waistband. She might as well have been naked for the shock that went sizzling through him.

Just then another streak of lightning lit up the room, her tousled hair, her pretty face with its huge and frightened eyes.

"Here." He got a better handle on her and lifted her up to the bunk, trying not to think about all the firm, smooth, fragrant flesh at his fingertips. "It'll be fine, Laura. Just go to sleep."

Easing back down on the mattress, Sam scrunched the pillow under his neck and stared straight up while he counted the seconds between the lightning hits and subsequent claps of thunder. Close, all of them. The damned storm seemed content just to hang right over his house. Directly above him, he heard Laura thrashing around, whipping the covers over her head, then following them with the pillow.

The next hit not only sounded as if it took out a tree, but it sent his bunkmate scrambling from hers down to his.

''Please, just hold me,'' she whispered even as she was slithering under the covers, into his arms, all warm and trembling against him.

A man would have to have a heart of stone to resist. Sam gathered her closer. ''It's all right, Laura, honey. I promise.''

''Make it stop,'' she whimpered.

Sam wished he could. He didn't know how to make her feel safe. All he knew was that suddenly he was kissing her trembling lips.

He was thinking to console her with soft, warm, little kisses, but they quickly escaped his control. And then he wasn't thinking at all, but was kissing her not so softly anymore, taking her mouth with a fierce need that ripped through him like the lightning that kept flashing again and again and again.

He kissed her until the fear in her voice turned to urgency, until her hands were reaching for him the way his were for her, until she breathed in his ear a deep and unmistakable *Oh, yes. Please. Now.* Then the storm outside seemed to come inside, to move through both of them as their bodies joined, fierce and wild, electric, sizzling, and impossibly, achingly complete.

With Sam's warm body covering hers and her face buried in the damp crook of his shoulder, Laura wasn't sure if it was still storming or not. The thunder pounding in her ears at the moment was the rush of her own blood. A kind of lightning had just snapped along every nerve in her body, leaving her exquisitely weak and deliciously wrung out.

When she stretched languidly, Sam immediately shifted his comforting weight.

"I'm sorry," he said. "Oh, God, I'm sorry. I don't know what came over me. That was…it was…"

"Wonderful," Laura said, still a little breathless, her body still reverberating like a bright silver bell.

"Well…yeah."

He sounded surprised, Laura thought. And when he levered up on an elbow and gazed down at her, a flash of lightning revealed a rather surprised, almost baffled expression on his face. The man who had just made love to her like a ravenous wolf appeared sheepish all of a sudden. Superman had reverted once more to adorable Clark Kent.

Laura didn't know whether to laugh or cry.

"What are you thinking?" she asked, regretting the question almost as soon as she spoke it, preferring to be blissfully ignorant just a little while longer.

But whatever it was that Sam was thinking, he didn't get the chance to tell her because just then somebody began pounding frantically on the front door downstairs.

Chapter 6

Laura stood in darkness near the top of the stairs, hugging a sheet around herself, listening to Sam trying to calm the hysterical woman who'd been knocking on the door. Poor Sam. That seemed to be his lot in life. Calming hysterical women. Tonight, at least.

As nearly as she could gather from Sam's questions and the sobbing responses, Janey Sayles's young daughter was very ill. The storm had knocked out Janey's electricity as well as her telephone. She didn't know what else to do.

"Help me, Sam."

"Where's Samantha now?"

"Out in the car. She needs to get to the hospital. Now."

"Are you sure it's serious, Janey?"

"Of course, I'm sure. What are you asking me, Sam? Why else would I be here for God's sake?"

"Okay. Okay. My vehicle's better than yours in

this weather. Can you move her while I get some clothes on?''

"Yes. She can still walk. At least, I think she can. Oh, hurry.''

The front door slammed and Sam raced up the dark staircase, nearly knocking Laura over when he reached the top.

"I heard,'' she said. "I'll get dressed. I'm going with you.''

When he started to discourage her, Laura practically growled, "If you think I'm going to stay here all by myself in this storm, Sam Zachary, then you better think again. Anyway, maybe I can help.''

"All right. Hurry up then.''

Laura was dressed before he was, and waiting for him at the front door. They ran through the fierce, slashing rain to the Blazer, and when Sam opened the rear door for her, Laura saw the precious little girl lying curled up and sucking her thumb in the back seat.

"Poor baby,'' she said, climbing in and settling herself carefully so as not to disturb the child.

"What are *you* doing here?'' Janey Sayles asked from the front seat. Then, when Sam got behind the wheel, the woman fairly snarled at him, "I don't believe this. What's *she* doing here?''

"She's coming with us.'' Sam twisted the key in the ignition, shifted, and stepped on the gas.

In the back seat, Laura shot out her hand to brace the little girl and prevent her from rolling onto the floor.

"Does she *have* to?'' Janey whined.

"Yes,'' Sam answered bluntly.

The woman aimed another dark glare toward the

back seat before she shrank down into the collar of her raincoat. It was quiet in the front seat then except for the whooshing of the wipers across the windshield and the continued reverberations of the thunderclaps.

Laura kept one hand on the little girl's shoulder, patting it reassuringly every so often. In the occasional flashes of lightning, she could see a pair of big brown eyes gazing up at her sleepily, but curiously.

"What's your name, sweetheart?" Laura asked softly.

The child's thumb popped out just long enough for her to respond, "'Mantha."

"'Mantha, hmm."

"Samantha," her mother hissed from the front. "Be still." The woman's glare shifted to Laura. "Leave her alone. She's much too sick to be talking."

Laura leaned down to whisper close to the child's ear. "That's a very pretty name, Samantha."

The little girl grinned for a second, her lips tilting up at the edges of her fist, then she frowned in her mother's direction and closed her eyes.

Laura wanted to ask her where she felt bad, but refrained, not wanting to cause any more ill feeling than she already had by her mere presence in the truck. Samantha didn't strike her as sick enough to require a visit to an emergency room. But what did she know? She wasn't a mother, after all.

She wasn't, was she?

Good Lord. Her gaze flitted to Sam's image in the rearview mirror. Serious. Sober. In total control. Not like before when they'd both lost every vestige of control. Neither one of them had used their heads, not to mention anything else earlier during their storm-tossed encounter, had they? It had happened so fast that she hadn't even had time to think.

Laura turned her face to the window and stared out into the wet dark night. Now, with ample time to consider the consequences of what she and Sam had done, she really didn't want to.

Ten minutes later, the Blazer skidded to a stop at the Emergency entrance of the Summit County hospital. Sam jumped out, wrenched open the back door, and scooped the little girl up in his arms. After his two-year stint as county sheriff, not to mention all of Janey's prior false alarms, he knew the drill.

"You can wait here if you want," he said to Laura. "This probably won't take long."

"I'll come in," she said. "Why don't I park the truck for you?"

"Great. Thanks. I left the keys in."

Janey gave his sleeve a hard tug. "Hurry, Sam."

He hurried through the sliding double doors, aware that his entrance would be greeted with muted groans from the ER staff and a silent chorus of "Here we go again." He didn't blame them a bit.

"You'll be fine, sweetheart," he whispered to Samantha as he passed her into the outstretched arms of Norma Jefferson, the charge nurse.

"What is it this time, Sam?" she asked with a slight roll of her eyes.

"She's running a fever," Janey said, edging between them. "Her head aches. Her throat is sore. And she keeps complaining that her neck hurts." She fixed her gaze fiercely on Samantha. "Don't you, baby? Tell them how your neck hurts. Tell them what you told Mommy earlier.''

"Does it, Samantha?'' Norma asked.

The child responded with a sleepy nod.

"Okay. Let's have Doctor Miller take a look at you. We'll put her in Room Three, Ms. Sayles. I think you know where that is.''

"Yes,'' Janey said. "Yes, of course, I do.''

She hooked her arm through Sam's and started forward, but Norma turned, speared Janey with a glare that only a charge nurse was capable of, and told her in no uncertain terms what she already knew—that only parents were allowed in the examining rooms.

"Oh, but...''

Sam eased his arm from Janey's grasp. "It'll be okay. I'll wait out here and get started on the paperwork for you.''

"Oh, but...''

"In here, Ms. Sayles,'' the nurse called.

"Go on.'' Sam gave her shoulders a gentle nudge to set her off down the little corridor with its curtained-off rooms.

"You'll wait for us, won't you, Sam?'' Janey asked over her shoulder.

He tried to disguise his sigh. He tried even harder to dredge up a smile. It wasn't all that easy. "Sure. Don't I always?''

In the deserted waiting room, Laura sat rubbing the rain off her arms and face when Sam came in with two cups of steaming coffee.

"Thanks for parking the truck,'' he said, holding

out one of the cups to her. "Here. I think this is the one without sugar."

Laura took a tiny, tentative sip. The coffee was piping hot and blessedly sugar free. "Perfect. Thanks. How's Samantha?"

He lowered himself into the chair next to hers. "She'll be fine."

"You sound pretty sure."

He sighed. "Well, this has happened before."

"Ah," Laura murmured noncommittally.

"Janey kind of panics. It's tough, I guess, being a single mother." He slung his long legs out, tipped his head back, and closed his eyes a moment.

Laura was tempted to say that she wouldn't know about that, but she dreaded their conversation getting anywhere near what had happened between them earlier. She glanced at the clock on the far wall. It was almost two. She wished she could turn back the hands. She wished it were midnight again, that she'd stayed in that top bunk, or better yet, remained in the room across the hall.

From the look of him, Sam was wishing the same thing. The set of his mouth was positively grim. Laura's heart did a surprising little flip as she remembered the feel of that mouth on hers, the taste of him, the sensuous glide of his tongue. She let out a long breath, banishing the memory as best she could.

A stern-looking nurse with a mouth as flat and grim as Sam's walked into the waiting room, waving a paper at him. "She's too upset, she says, to fill out the rest of this. Here you go, Sam." The woman rolled her eyes as she thrust the printed form into Sam's hand. "Again."

"How's Samantha?" he asked.

"Oh, fine. No fever. No rash. Except Janey won't quit about the stiff neck, so we'll have to do a spinal tap on the poor little kid just to be on the safe side and rule out meningitis."

"Meningitis!" Laura gasped.

The nurse looked at her as if suddenly realizing Laura was sitting there. "Are you a relative?"

"No. Just...just a friend."

"I didn't realize Janey had any friends," she said sourly, before turning back to Sam. "Doctor Singh is doing an emergency appendectomy right now, so it'll be at least two more hours."

"Okay," Sam said wearily. "Thanks, Norma. If you've got a pen, I'll just start filling this out."

She plucked a ballpoint from her pocket and handed it to him. "Oh, and Sam?"

"Yeah?"

Her taut lips slid into a tiny, teasing grin. "I really hate to be the one to tell you this, but just to be on the safe side, since you may have been exposed to meningitis, we're going to have to give both you and the lady here an antibiotic shot."

Laura heard Sam swallow audibly, almost painfully before he responded, "Yeah. Okay. No problem, Norma."

"I'll let you know when we're ready." She walked away laughing.

"What was that all about?" Laura asked, thinking her Superman was looking decidedly queasy. "Why was she laughing like that?"

"I don't know," he said. He put his coffee down on a table, reached for a magazine to brace the paper on his leg, then clicked the ballpoint open decisively before adding, "I guess she just knows how much I hate filling out forms."

Laura didn't think that was exactly the case from the way Sam dived into it, filling boxes with perfect little *X*s and moving methodically from line to line, his printing dark and squarish and wonderfully neat, as legible as the printed form itself. In contrast, Janey's thin and shaky scrawl across the upper part of the page was practically impossible to read.

Well, except for what she'd written on the line under Name of Father. Laura leaned a little bit closer just to make certain she'd read it correctly. She squinted. No, there was absolutely no mistaking what Janey had written there. Name of Father: Zachary, Samuel Ulysses.

That stunning bit of information had barely registered on her brain when Norma whisked into the waiting room once more.

"It's time for Mr. Needle, Sam," she announced, thumping the clipboard in her hand. "Cindy's waiting for you in Room Two. Let's go, big guy."

"Very funny," Sam grumbled, getting up. He clicked the pen closed. "Here's your form, all filled out."

Norma took the paper and pen from him. "Room Two," she said again. "Go on. I need to get a couple signatures from this lady and then she'll be right behind you."

Sam started to say something to Laura, but the nurse cut him off with a stern, "Now, Sam."

"Right. Okay. I'm going. See you, Laura."

As soon as Sam headed for the door, Norma plopped down in his vacant chair, crossed her white-stockinged legs, and shoved her clipboard toward

Laura. "I'll need you to sign your name here and here and down here," she said briskly, pointing her pen at three separate lines on some forms. "These are just our standard releases for treatment. They're no big deal."

"All right." Laura studied them briefly, then held out her hand for the pen.

While she signed, the nurse leaned closer. "Listen, since you're a friend of Janey's, maybe you can talk to her and get her to lighten up on Sam."

"Lighten up?" She glanced up at the woman, whose expression looked earnest, completely sincere.

"This is the sixth time Janey's dragged him here this year alone. She's a wacko, a total nutcase, but Sam can't see it. And the poor guy just doesn't know how to say no where little Samantha's concerned."

Laura finished off her final signature with a flourish and handed the clipboard back to Norma.

Good God. Didn't this woman read her damned forms? Didn't she know that Sam was Samantha's father? As for *dragging* poor ol' beleaguered Sam, Laura wanted to suggest twenty miles behind a buckboard through a cactus-rich environment. And that was just for starters.

She'd been so wrong about Sam's character. She'd been so sure that he was different. Better. A real hero.

"It's really none of my business," she said as coolly as she could.

"Okay. Well, I figured it couldn't hurt to ask," Norma said. "Somebody really ought to do something about that woman before..."

Laura stood up. "If I have to have a shot, I'd like to get it over with as soon as possible, please."

The nurse sighed. "Sure. Okay. Follow me."

They crossed the brightly lit entrance foyer again, then turned down the small corridor with curtained-off cubicles. Outside of one of these, Laura saw at least half a dozen hospital employees in white uniforms and green scrubs gathered.

"Must be some emergency in there," she said.

"That?" Norma gestured to the little knot of nurses and orderlies. "That's no emergency. It's just Sam."

"Sam? I don't understand. Is something wrong?"

"No," she said. "Nothing's wrong. They're just betting which way he'll fall when he goes down like a tree."

Laura blinked. "Excuse me?"

"The shot. Oh, I guess you wouldn't know. Sam has a tendency to faint." She grinned as she whisked back the curtain on an adjacent cubicle. "Here you go. I'll be right back. I need to get my bet in."

"Very funny, guys." Sam was unbuckling his belt. "You night shift ghouls are pretty easily entertained, if you ask me."

"My money's on right, Sheriff," a male voice called from the corridor. "Don't you do one of those slow knee sinkers, now."

"If I were still sheriff, Luther, I'd bust you for gambling," Sam called back gruffly even as he smiled to himself.

Damned if he knew why needles literally brought him to his knees. They'd never bothered him when he was a kid, but after he was inducted into the Marine Corps and spent nearly an entire day getting inoculated, passing out, getting up again only to be shot once more, hypodermic needles had become the bane of his existence.

During his service in the Corps, and particularly during his stint as county sheriff, he'd seen enough blood and gore to last a lifetime. Gunshot wounds. Stabbings. Accident victims with every sort of fracture imaginable. A plane crash where the pilot and two passengers were burned beyond recognition. None of those brought him down the way a tiny little needle did. Even the idea of one.

His skin was already prickling with a cold sweat. There was enough of a tremor in his hands that he wasn't entirely sure he could unsnap or unzip his jeans.

"Just about ready, Sam," Cindy said from the counter where she was preparing her instrument of torture.

"Yeah. Okay."

"Which cheek you gonna stick, Cindy?" Luther called.

"I don't know," she answered, her back still turned, her shoulders shaking with merciless, even sadistic laughter. "I'm open to suggestions."

"Right," Luther shouted.

"Left," somebody else said.

"Sam?" Cindy turned, the hypodermic needle held high while she squirted a pale stream of fluid upward. The little blonde was grinning like a jack-o-lantern. "Left or right?"

"Right," he said, proving that even though he was a coward, he was not a man of indecision. While his shaking fingers dealt with the snap and the zipper, he tried to remember the color of the briefs he'd pulled on earlier in the darkness, praying those wouldn't add to his humiliation. God. Let them be black. Or white. Not the purple ones. Please.

"He's going a little green on me, guys," Cindy called out. "I think somebody ought to come in here and take an elbow, at least."

Then Luther's smiling face swam up in Sam's vision. "Sam. My man. Be cool."

Sam wasn't.

The last thing he remembered was Luther muttering, "Damn. A sinker. Straight down at the knees."

Laura sat on a cinder block wall just outside the emergency room. It had stopped raining, thank God, but all the inclemency seemed to have transferred itself to her current mood. She almost wished she were a smoker. This would have been the perfect time to light up, to shake out a hot match and then exhale an angry blast of smoke.

She really didn't want to go home with Sam, but she really, really didn't want to go back to her apartment, either, until she figured out how to deal with Artie. She was considering calling a cab and going to a motel when Clark Kent came through the sliding glass doors, seemingly none the worse for his recent encounter with Kryptonite.

"Are you okay?" she asked, even though she didn't care all that much.

"Oh," he said. "I guess you heard."

She shrugged. "Well, I was in the room right next to yours."

When he dragged his fingers through his hair, grinned sheepishly, and murmured, "What a wuss, huh?" she almost felt sorry for him. Almost.

"Everybody's scared of something," she said.

"Oh, yeah?" His warm brown eyes—glittery in the vapor lights from the nearby parking lot—fixed intently on her face. "What are you scared of, Laura McNeal?" Without shifting his gaze, he nudged his chin toward the sky. "Other than lightning and thunder, I mean."

You, she wanted to say while her lips twitched silently. I'm scared of the way my heart drops to my stomach when you look at me. The way my body feels when you touch me with those big, competent hands of yours. The feeling of safety that somehow seeps into me when I'm near you. You, Sam. I'm scared to death of you.

"Artie," she said finally, hugging her arms about her as if taken by a sudden chill. "I'm scared of Artie, but you already know that."

"You should be," he said, "but you don't have to worry about him. I can't do anything about the weather, Laura, but I *will* take care of that punk for you." He held out one big, competent hand. "Come on. I'm beat. Let's go home."

Home. The word came out all cozy and warm, all snug as a bug in a rug under windows with lace curtains, all porch swing and rose trellis and vegetable garden. The home where his daughter ought to be.

"What about Samantha?" she asked, disregarding the outstretched hand with what she hoped was obvious disdain.

"They're keeping her overnight for observation. She'll be fine. Her mother's staying with her."

"I see."

No, she didn't see at all. She'd never understand how fathers could walk away from their little girls.

How they could not write, not call, not come back. Ever.

"Okay. Let's go," she said, shoving off the wall and striding toward the spot where she'd parked his Blazer. At the passenger door, she dug in her handbag for the keys. "Here." She plopped them into his hand.

After Sam opened the door for her, Laura quickly hoisted herself into the seat before he could even think of assisting her. When he climbed in, he stuck the key in the ignition, but didn't turn it. Instead, he sat back and blew out a soft curse.

"Laura, about what happened tonight...with us..."

"I don't want to talk about it."

"It's just that..."

"I said I don't want to talk about it, Sam." She practically growled. How was she going to pretend it never happened if he kept bringing it up? How could she forget she'd just made one of the biggest mistakes in her life if he was going to keep reminding her?

"Let's just go. Okay?"

"Okay." He started the truck, but before he put it in gear, he said quietly, "I'm so damned sorry."

"Fine," she snapped. "Apology accepted. You're sorry. I'm even sorrier. It'll never happen again. Now let's just for heaven's sake go."

Let it go, Sam told himself while he focused on the far reach of the headlights down the dark road. Laura had accepted his apology. It wouldn't happen again. Just let it the hell go.

Laura rode beside him, arms crossed, legs crossed,

and for all he knew her eyes crossed, too. She didn't need to speak. Her body language fairly screamed *I despise you* as she sat hunkered down in the seat, chewing on her lip, staring straight ahead like someone who wished she were someplace else, or at the very least, *with* somebody else. Anybody but him.

Who could blame her? The guy who was supposed to take care of her had taken advantage of her instead. What a prince! What a knight in tarnished armor he'd turned out to be. The fact that he'd also been unfaithful to Jenny for the first time in his life wasn't something he could even deal with at the moment.

The Blazer's big tires crunched on the wet gravel of the driveway when he turned in and the high beams illuminated a blue pickup truck parked askew, as if its driver had stepped hard on the brakes, jumped out and left the door open.

"Oh, great. This is just great," Sam said. Even as he spoke, he could see Wes Gunther coming up off the porch swing and down the steps like he'd been shot out of a damned cannon.

"Who's that?" Laura asked, at last breaking her silence.

"That," Sam said wearily, "is Samantha's father, looking to bust my chops for the five hundredth time."

Chapter 7

Sam had ordered Laura to stay in the truck with the doors locked, but he hadn't said anything about not cracking a window so she could hear the shouting match currently taking place just a few yards from her ringside seat. She could see it clearly, too, because the storm had passed, the electricity had come back on, and the porch light on Sam's house cast a wide yellow swath across the wet front lawn where the two combatants stood.

Wes Gunther wore a grease-stained mechanic's jumpsuit with his name stitched prominently above one pocket. He was in his mid-thirties, Laura guessed, with long, dishwater hair pulled back and banded in a ratty ponytail. The man was a good three or four inches shorter than Sam and at least forty pounds lighter, but what he lacked in stature, he more than made up for in volume.

He was drunk, too. Very drunk. Laura didn't even

have to see the brown beer bottle clenched in his fist to know that.

"You just can't leave them alone, can you, Sam?" Wes bellowed. "Not Janey and not my kid. The minute the hospital called me tonight, I knew it was you there with them instead of me. Hell, it's always you instead of me."

"Now wait a minute, Wes," Sam answered calmly. "I didn't do..."

"No." The man lofted his arms dramatically and shook his head. "You didn't *do* anything. Hell, Sam, you never have to. You're just *here*. That's good enough for Janey."

His bleary gaze drifted toward the driveway and fixed on Laura in the front seat. His expression grew so belligerent that she felt like squirming down, safely out of sight.

"Who's that woman in your truck?" Wes yelled.

"A client," Sam answered.

"Oh, right. Sure she is. Does Janey know?"

"Yeah."

The man rolled his eyes and snorted. "Yeah, and I'll bet she's madder'n hell about it, too. Am I right? Damn right, I'm right."

Sam shrugged. "Janey's like a sister to me. You know that."

"She was Jenny's freaking sister, not yours. But you've gotta have 'em both, Sam, don't you? Huh? One's not good enough for you. Isn't that right?"

"Look, Wes. Maybe we should talk about this tomorrow." Sam crossed his arms and widened his stance. "I'm beat and you're skunked. That doesn't make for very intelligent conversation."

Wes lifted his bottle, tilted back his head and took

a long, wet pull, then he wiped his mouth with the back of his grease-streaked hand. "I didn't come over here tonight to have a goddamned conversation. Intelligent or otherwise. I came over here to bust your nose."

"Well, somebody's already done that," Sam said, "and it didn't solve any problems. It just hurt like hell, Wes, and I'm really not in the mood."

"Tough." The man took another sloppy swig, then drew back his arm and pitched the bottle at Sam's head.

Laura gasped. Sam ducked, and the bottle landed with a thunk on the wet grass. But no sooner had he straightened up than Wes Gunther howled like a wild, wounded animal and came charging at him.

Oh, God, Laura thought. Be careful, Sam.

She really ought to get out and help him, even if he had told her in no uncertain terms to stay in the truck. She scanned the yard for a fallen tree branch or a board, anything she might be able to use as a weapon. When her panicky gaze returned to the two combatants, however, it was obvious that Sam wasn't going to need help from Laura or anybody else.

He just stood where he was, solid as a tree, deflecting the rampaging Wes with his forearm, and at the same time sticking out his foot to trip the man and send him stumbling, then sprawling facedown on the rain-soaked lawn.

"Go home, Wes," Sam told him. "Sleep it off. We can talk about this tomorrow."

Swearing, Wes struggled to his knees, then lurched to his feet. He wiped his wet hands on the front of his jumpsuit, then fisted them again, growling, "I'm done talking to you, you son of a bitch."

He charged Sam again. And again.

From Laura's vantage point, the attack seemed to turn into a kind of boisterous, misbegotten ballet where one partner stood perfectly balanced, graceful and still in the yellow spotlight, while the other dancer slipped and slid and pinwheeled all around him. For every wild punch, there was a controlled countermove. For every ungainly lunge, there was a deft and perfect parry. For all of Wes's clumsiness, there was Sam's astonishing grace.

And then, while Laura watched mesmerized, it appeared that Sam grew tired of the confrontation, or bored with it perhaps, because the next time Wes lunged at him, Sam calmly doubled up his fist and landed a blow that dropped his attacker like a hundred-seventy-five-pound sack of potatoes. Wes went down, down and out like a light, at Sam's feet.

Laura scrambled out of the car. By the time she reached him, Sam had already picked up the unconscious man beneath his arms and was dragging him across the lawn.

"I'm sorry about this," he said. "Wes is a good guy, but he gets a few beers under his belt and he thinks he's Muhammad Ali."

"He's Samantha's father?" She looked down at the man's expressionless face in search of any resemblance to the child. There was none that she could see except perhaps for the color and texture of their hair.

"Apparently. He claims he is, anyway." Sam shrugged. "It's a long story, Laura, and it's three o'clock in the morning. I'm going to put ol' Wes in his truck, and then I'm going up to bed. You should probably do the same."

She should, Laura thought, but there was something she had to do first. "Sam," she called, following him across the lawn and along the driveway. "Sam, I want to apologize."

"Whatever it is, I accept."

Still holding Wes's inert body, he reached into the truck's interior through the open door, extracted the keys from the ignition, and lobbed them a good thirty or forty feet down the driveway. "There. That ought to keep him here till he sobers up enough to drive."

Then, juggling his burden of deadweight in order to open the pickup's door wider, Sam continued to ignore Laura.

"You can't just accept a person's apology until you know what it's for," she said.

"Yes, I can."

The words came out as a kind of grunt as he lifted Wes and maneuvered him onto the front seat, then slammed the door on him.

"No, you can't," she insisted.

"Yes," he said with a sort of deadly calm. "I can." Then he nudged her out of his way and began striding across the lawn.

Laura caught up with him when he bent to retrieve Wes's beer bottle. "Dammit, Sam. Will you please listen to me?"

He stood, towering over her, with the empty bottle in his left hand and his right hand ripping through his hair. Then he closed his eyes and let out a beleaguered, far from patient groan. "What?"

"I was angry with you earlier because..."

A growl rumbled deep in his throat, then he dropped the bottle and he reached out, pulling her against him, her face nearly scrunched in his shirt, effectively cutting off her speech.

"It's three o'clock in the damned morning, Laura. I can't even think straight anymore, but I distinctly remember apologizing for...you know...taking unfair advantage of you. If you still want to beat me up about it, that's fine, but can you please for God's sake wait until tomorrow to do it? How about noon? Would that work for you?"

When Laura made a muffled sound in his shirtfront, he loosened his arms and lifted one hand to tip her face up to his. Much to her surprise, he looked far more sweet than sour, even if there was a certain gruffness in his voice when he said, "Look, if it's any kind of consolation, that was probably the best sex I've ever had in my entire life. My body's still ringing like a goddamned tuning fork."

Laura blinked as she inhaled a startled little breath. "It is?"

"Yeah." A little grin pulled at his lips, and his gruff voice softened to a whisper. "Yes, it is."

"Mine, too."

Sam's gaze, hungry all of a sudden, hot and ravenous, dropped to her mouth, sending Laura's heart into a breathless free-fall. His arms tightened around her, and a low, almost helpless curse was still reverberating on his lips when they took full and fierce possession of hers.

At nine o'clock the next morning, Sam sat on the porch swing sipping hot, sugar-laced coffee, burning his tongue, accepting that as just desserts for his unbelievably stupid and lecherous behavior the night before. All told, he figured he'd had about seven minutes of solid sleep in between all the tossing and turning and pillow punching, not to mention the guilt and recriminations. This morning, when Wes fired up the engine of his truck and peeled out of the driveway at half past eight, Sam gave up any attempt to go back to sleep.

He still wasn't sure what had come over him last night. Less than an hour after he'd promised Laura it would never happen again, it happened again. God bless it. He hadn't even meant to kiss her, but suddenly there she was looking up at him with her big blue velvet eyes and a wet shine on her lips that obliterated every civilized thought in his brain.

He practically tore her clothes off right there on the front lawn. Then—in a brief moment of blessed sanity—he carried her, long legs wrapped around his hips, arms wound tightly around his neck, into the house where they hadn't even made it up the stairs. Hell, they hadn't even made it as far as the sofa, but made wild, unbridled, white-hot love on the hardwood living-room floor. He thought he might have broken the stubborn zipper on Laura's jeans. He knew for a fact that he'd popped at least two buttons on his shirt when he'd wrenched it off over his head.

Shaking his head as much in disgust as disbelief, Sam took another sip of the sweet, searing coffee. He wasn't that kind of man. He wasn't a shirt-wrenching, zipper-breaking, bra-tugging, silk-and-lace-ripping animal. At least he never had been until Laura McNeal worked whatever brand of witchcraft she was using on him. Before now, before *her,* he'd never even considered himself a very sexual person.

In all their time together, he and Jenny had gone to bed more as an afterthought than anything else.

Making love just hadn't been that important, not in the grand scheme of their relationship. If it ever had been important to him, he'd either suppressed those feelings or altered them to match Jenny's cooler temperament.

She was so tiny, his Jenny, so fine-boned and delicate, and he was always so damned afraid of hurting her that it almost became a relief to hear her say *Not tonight, Sam.*

In their final two or three years together, Jenny had said that a lot. He'd gotten used to passion in a minor key. He liked it that way. At least, he'd told himself he did. But suddenly here he was, full of thundering chords and red-hot jazz, a kind of primal music he didn't like one bit.

He didn't want this. After Jenny's death, getting involved with a woman was the farthest thing from Sam's mind. If he'd wanted an involvement, if he'd craved any kind of female companionship at all, there was always Janey, waiting patiently on his doorstep, clearly his for the taking.

Or maybe not so patient, he thought. Drunk as he'd been last night, Wes Gunther was absolutely right. Sam had to do something about Janey. But what? He had to do something about Laura, too, but he'd be damned if he knew what. He was mulling over his options when Laura called to him from inside the house.

He found her in the kitchen, on the phone. She was wearing—heaven help him—one of his plaid flannel shirts, the tail of which barely succeeded in covering hers. And there, below the shirttail, were those long, lean, mesmerizing legs. That predictable, improbable, uncontrollable heat rushed through him again. Get a grip, he warned himself. You're not that kind of man.

When she turned and saw him, she immediately handed him the receiver.

"I've called a cab," she said, "but I don't know how to give them directions. Would you, please?"

"A cab?" he asked stupidly, holding the phone as if it were some mysterious object. A moon rock. A fossil. A hunk of strange debris.

"I want to go home, Sam."

"I'll take you. You don't…"

"No." She shook her head. "Please just tell the woman at the cab company how to get to your house."

Sam lifted the phone to his ear, started to mumble about highways and bridges and intersections, then gave the dispatcher a gruff "Never mind" and slapped the receiver back on the phone.

"What did you do that for?"

Because I'm an idiot, he thought. There was no other explanation.

"I don't want you going back to your place alone, Laura," he said. "You hired me to help you, and that's what I'm going to do."

"Well, I've decided to unhire you." She blew a stray wisp of hair off her forehead. "You're not helping me, Sam. You're not helping me at all. You're just…I don't know…confusing me."

She raised her arms in a helpless gesture that succeeded mostly in confusing Sam because he didn't know whether to look at her exposed thighs or her eyes. His gaze kind of floundered from one to the other.

"What are you confused about?" he asked lamely.

"Me. You. Us. Well, sex, if you want the absolute truth. I don't usually…I'm not…oh, hell."

Her pretty face was so squinched up in frustration that it almost made Sam laugh. Except there was nothing funny about what she'd just said. That was the same way he was feeling. Oh, hell summed it up pretty well.

"I don't usually, and I'm not, either," he said with a little laugh that sounded more like indigestion than amusement. "I'm pretty confused myself."

"You!"

She had turned to pour a cup of coffee, and with her exclamation, poured more coffee onto the counter than into her cup. "It seems to me your only confusion lies in deciding just how many women you can keep dangling on your string."

"That's not true."

"Isn't it?"

With her back still to him, she snapped a paper towel off the holder and gave a vicious swipe to the countertop. "Well, let's see. There's ol' Janey, who's so thoroughly hooked that she won't even give you up for the father of her child. There's me, and it only took you about twenty-four hours to get me into bed. Twice, I might add. There certainly must be somebody else."

"There's nobody else."

After dropping the crumpled paper towel in the trash can, she turned to face him. "I'm just not in your league, Sam. That's all I'm saying. I'm not the kind of person who falls into bed with a man after only knowing him for a day or two." She rolled her eyes. "Well, at least I didn't used to be. There! You see? You've got me so confused I don't even know what kind of person I am anymore."

He didn't know what to say. A wan shrug was the best he could offer at the moment. It was either that or wrapping his arms around her, and he didn't think that was a very wise move under the circumstances.

Laura continued, pacing back and forth in front of the sink, her coffee sloshing in its cup. "Not only that, but I don't know what kind of signals I'm giving off these days. First there was Artie with all his unsolicited gifts and his proposal and his unsolicited fist. Then you, all of a sudden, with that mesmerizing mouth of yours and those great hands and your...well...my God." Her eyes rolled toward the ceiling again.

He still didn't know what to say, and a second shrug seemed way too cavalier. An embrace was still out of the question.

"I just want to go home," she said, putting the cup down, shaking her head. "I just need to go home. Now. Right now."

What he wanted to say was *Stay,* but instead he said, "Okay. I'll take you home."

Laura watched the farms and green fields gradually give way to strip malls and office complexes. It was the reverse of their drive just two days ago, but she felt as if she'd been away far longer than that. Weeks. Even months.

She stared silently out the window, remembering how she'd worried during that earlier drive that Sam might turn down some country road and attack her. Little did she know that when the time came she'd be such an eager participant. Not once, but twice, for heaven's sake.

Sam Zachary, despite his vegetable garden and his ruffled, blue gingham apron and fussy culinary skills, was an amazing lover. Urgent. Ardent. All-consuming. Laura glanced to her left, at his hands on the steering wheel, those strong, sure hands that had done such incredible things to her body the night before. She tried to remember the name of the song he had played on the piano. "Liebestraum." That was it. Dream of Love. She couldn't have dreamed it any better.

No one had ever made love to her with such passion. Not that she was an expert, or required even a whole hand of fingers to count her previous lovers. There had only been one, and it had taken an engagement ring and more than a little persuasion plus a good deal of champagne to get her into bed. Not like Sam. Not a bit like Sam.

Laura had promised herself she'd never dream of love again. Then Sam had played her like "Liebestraum" last night. Twice.

This morning she'd awakened, her mind still half dazed and her body deliciously sore, and decided then and there that she'd rather take her chances with Artie than spend one more day with Sam. When it came right down to it, a broken bone didn't sound half so bad as a broken heart.

There was already a jagged stress fracture in that poor organ, for despite all his protests, Sam had finally agreed to take her home. They were only a few blocks away when she asked, "Do I owe you any more money?"

"No," he said irritably, not taking his eyes off the

street ahead. "In fact I should probably give you a refund. I didn't exactly solve your problem for you."

"That's okay. It's *my* problem. I'll figure out a way to handle it. And anyway, you've got enough problems of your own."

Even as she spoke, Laura was wondering what Sam was going to do about Janey and Wes and their little girl. The fissure in her heart cracked a little bit more when she realized that she'd probably never know, that what had seemed like her concern for a day or two, really wasn't any of her business at all.

"I hope everything works out for you, Sam," she said, meaning it with all her heart. "If you ever decide to get rid of your mother's clothes, why don't you give me a call? I could sell them on consignment for you, or I could just buy them from you outright. Whatever you prefer."

"Maybe," he said, scowling as he spoke and sounding more as if he meant probably not.

He stopped the Blazer at the light, then turned the corner of Stevenson Boulevard onto shabby Russell Avenue where Nana's Attic was located just two blocks east. Laura still felt as if she'd been gone more than a few days. Rolling her window down, she drew in a long breath of exhaust fumes and blistering tar and dumpsters. Ah, the fragrance of home. Who needed clean country air?

She noticed a hand-written Going Out Of Business sign in the window of Stemmler's Drug Store, and she was sure the notice hadn't been there when she left. Still, it didn't surprise her. Art Hammerman, who owned nearly every building on both sides of the street and was hatching a plan for an inner-city upscale shopping street, had probably raised Mr.

Stemmler's rent another notch and this time succeeded in driving the poor old man out of business. The Hammer had struck again.

Nana's Attic, sitting smack in the middle of the block, was undoubtedly somewhere on his list. Laura was wondering just how long she had before he raised her rent sky-high and drove her out of business, too. It was a shame, really, that Artie was such a creep because a relationship with the Hammer's son could have been so beneficial.

She was thinking that, instead of hiring a private eye, she would have been a lot better off picking up a copy of *How to Swim with the Sharks,* when she heard Sam's sudden and sharp intake of breath. When she looked down the block in the direction of his gaze, all Laura could see was a fire engine parked in the street, right in front of where her building used to be.

Chapter 8

"**Y**ou're absolutely sure it was lightning?" Sam asked the fire marshal, a big-bellied, blue-uniformed, brass-buttoned man who seemed much more concerned at the moment about the condition of his shoeshine than the gutted building directly in front of him.

"That was one hell of a storm last night," the man said, giving a last woeful look at his soaked and grimy brogans. "Hell of a storm. Lightning hit the roof of Saint Stephen's, too." He pointed a stubby index finger. "Got this building right there at the southwest corner."

"There were witnesses?" Sam asked.

The fire marshal aimed a thumb toward a place called Hal and Sandy's on the opposite side of the street. "Yeah. Several," he said, "and not all of them three sheets to the wind. It was lightning, all right. No doubt about it."

That came as an enormous relief to Sam, whose immediate suspicion and worst fear had been that Laura's erstwhile friend and stalker, Artie, might have been responsible for the blaze. He was grateful that wasn't the case, but at the same time he dreaded telling Laura, as afraid of storms as she was, that a random bolt of lightning had had her name on it last night.

Jesus. At least she hadn't been there when it struck. He wondered if it had happened while they were making love, a literal lightning strike comparable to the figurative one he had felt when he exploded inside her, a jolt that had left him feeling a little like the smoking rubble in front of him now.

"You live here?" the fire marshal asked.

"No. A friend. She wasn't here last night."

"Lucky."

"Yeah." Sam rolled his shoulders to ease the tension there. "She's waiting in my Blazer over there. She's pretty upset. This was her business as well as her residence. You need any information from her?"

"Just a routine form filled out since she wasn't the property's owner. She can mail it to us. Hang on. I'll get one from my car."

Sam looked back at what was left of Laura's building. Not much. They were getting ready to pull the rear wall down so it didn't collapse onto the alley. The second-floor apartment—Laura's home—was gone. The first-floor shop was gone, as well. Everything above street level, every stick of furniture, every item of clothing, every board and cross-beam, was now reduced to cinders in the soggy wreckage of the basement.

He walked through the maze of fire hoses on the

wet pavement, back to where Laura waited in his truck. He leaned down, bracing his forearms on the window opening.

"It's totaled," he said. "Nothing's salvageable, Laura. I'm really sorry."

She was pale, and her blank gaze was similar to the hundred-yard stare of a soldier in battle.

"I have insurance," she said weakly. "I mailed in a payment just a couple of weeks ago. I'm sure I did."

"That's good," he murmured, hoping hard that her next question wouldn't be about the origin of the fire.

"Can't I even pick through what's left? I might... There might be something..."

"Too dangerous, honey." He leaned a little farther in the window to softly touch her cheek. "There's nothing. Trust me. They're going to bulldoze it and haul it away tomorrow."

She was biting her lower lip to keep it from trembling. "I just can't believe this. Did...did they say how it started? Do they have any idea?"

Sam closed his eyes a minute. God, he didn't want to tell her it was lightning. That might really freak her out.

"Was it arson?" she asked.

He shook his head.

"I'm sure it was," she said. "It had to be Artie."

Now he didn't know which would be worse, letting her believe that her stalker was capable of such a vicious crime or telling her about the lightning. Laura spared him that decision, however, with her next question. It came out somewhere between a wail and a wet, pitiful sigh.

"What am I going to do? Where am I going to go?"

Home, he thought, with me. But he didn't dare say it. "Can you stay with relatives? Friends?"

"The only relative I have is a cousin in California, and the only friend I could impose on like that moved to Kansas two years ago." She knuckled away a tear. "Pretty pitiful, huh?"

Sam drew in a breath. "You could always impose on me." What the hell, he thought. The worst she could say was no.

"Yes."

Laura's lips had been about to frame a distinct and unequivocal *no* when the sleek black stretch limo turned the corner half a block away and glided to a stop in front of what used to be her building.

The license plate read Hammer-l, not that anybody needed to see the plate to know who the vehicle belonged to or who sat in the back seat behind those smoked glass windows. Chances were good that Artie sat there, too, accompanying his father on this inspection of their devastated property. Ha! Returning to the scene of the crime was more like it.

"If it wouldn't be too much of an imposition, Sam," she said, sliding down in the seat, trying to make herself small if not invisible. "At least until I can come up with something else."

"Great," he said, blinking and looking a bit surprised.

But hardly more surprised than Laura was herself. Going back to Sam's house was the last thing she ever thought she'd be doing today. Or ever.

"Could we go right now?" she asked, peeking

over the dashboard, watching the Hammer's driver and his bodyguard emerge, one from each side of the front seat.

"Uh...sure. Absolutely. Let me just talk to the fire marshal a second. He's got some form he needs you to fill out. I'll be right back."

"Okay."

Hurry, she wanted to add, watching the bodyguard's hand reach for the handle on the limo's rear door, not knowing who would emerge or what would happen next. Whoever emerged, though, Laura figured he'd be smiling. Art Hammerman, Sr., had just acquired another empty lot to advance his shopping mall scheme. Junior, the creep, had just revenged himself on the woman who had scorned him, not to mention furthering dear old dad's investment plans. The Hammermans, large and small, had really scored big on this one.

Hurry, Sam, she thought, watching him amble along the wet sidewalk past the limo toward the bright red fire marshal's vehicle. He was nearly shoulder to shoulder with the Hammer's bodyguard, and Laura couldn't help but notice that her own bodyguard looked quite capable of taking the other man, at least two out of three.

She let out a tiny sigh of relief, but sucked it right back in when the Hammer, in his shiny gray sharkskin suit, oozed out of the limo's back seat, stood on the sidewalk a moment readjusting his French cuffs, then promptly shook hands with Sam!

Laura's heart slammed against her ribs. She slid down farther in the seat, hugged her arms tightly about herself and squeezed her eyes closed. This couldn't be happening. The Hammer was shaking hands with Sam. They were greeting each other like long lost buddies. Brothers reunited. Siamese twins rejoined at the wrist. What in the world did that mean? It couldn't be anything good. It had to be horrible. What the hell was she supposed to do now?

The instant he reached out to grasp Art Hammerman's hairy paw, all the puzzle pieces came together in Sam's brain and he felt like using his other hand to slap his forehead. Artie! He should have known. Laura's landlord's son was no Jones. He was Artie Hammerman, junior thug. No wonder Laura was terrified. No wonder she had to work her way down to the *Zs* in the Yellow Pages before she could find somebody who would help her.

"It's Sam, right? Sam Zachary, the P.I.?" the Hammer asked in his gravelly movie-gangster voice.

Sam never had been able to figure out if that rasp was natural or affected. Either way, it worked sufficiently to make Art Hammerman, at a lowly five foot eight in his elevator shoes, sound more like six foot two.

"Right. Sam Zachary. How're you doing, Mr. Hammerman?"

"You know this guy, boss?" the beefy bodyguard asked, moving in closer while he looked Sam over from head to toe.

"Yeah, Joey. Don't worry about it. He's okay. Just a guy who did a little work for me a couple of years ago." Hammerman gave Sam a squinty look. "It was no big deal, right?"

"No big deal," Sam said with a shrug, even though, as deals went, it had been fairly big when the man with his fingers in just about every pie in town had hired him on the sly a year or so ago to do a little surveillance of the very young, very beautiful, and—as it turned out—very unfaithful Mrs. Hammerman. Well, judging from what Sam read in the papers, the very ex-Mrs. Hammerman now.

"Damned shame, huh?" The Hammer was gesturing toward the smoldering ruins. "Glad nobody got hurt." He snapped his gold-ringed, manicured fingers in the direction of the bodyguard. "What was the name of that secondhand clothes place? Grandma's something or other? You remember, Joey. That pretty little blonde Artie was so nuts about?"

"Nana's something," the burly man said, almost blushing. "I dunno, boss. Nana's something. Attic, I think."

"Yeah, that was it," the Hammer said. "Cute little blonde. She always paid her rent on time, too. See about sending her some flowers, Joey."

"Right, boss."

The Hammer gazed back at the wet pile of debris and gave a little shrug. "Hell of a thing. So, what brings you into this neighborhood, Sam?"

"The usual. I'm on a job."

"So, how's it going? Business good?"

"It comes and goes," Sam said. "I can't complain." Nor did Sam want to discuss his current client or Art, Jr.'s, alleged penchant for violence. Not until he found out the whole story. The puzzle pieces may have come together, but the picture still wasn't absolutely clear.

"Lightning," the mobster said, shaking his head as he pondered the wreckage of his property. "A bolt of lightning. What do you know about that?"

"Arson, compliments of Mother Nature," Sam murmured.

The Hammer chuckled. "Ain't that the truth?" He stuck out his hand. "Good seeing you, Sam. Gimme a call if you're ever looking for work."

"Will do, Mr. Hammerman. Good seeing you, too."

The man gave an affable, almost princely wave in the direction of the fire marshal, called out "Thanks, boys," then eased himself into the dark, luxurious confines of the back seat. A second after that, the limo doors closed with one soft thunk after another, the engine purred to life and the long vehicle slid into reverse and disappeared the way it had come.

Sam picked up the form from the fire marshal and walked slowly back to his truck, thinking pretty little Laura had more than a few blanks to fill in.

This time, when the Blazer turned down the tree-canopied lane, Laura was barely aware of the pastoral views on each side or the cows dotting the lush green fields or the birds perched so quaintly along the fence posts. She hadn't even asked Sam how he knew Art Hammerman. She didn't want to think about that or what it might mean. In fact, she was trying not to think at all because every time she did, she felt sick. Everything was gone. Everything.

The fact that she had insurance was a relief, but it wasn't much consolation at the moment. She didn't want new stuff. She wanted her old stuff. The priceless and irreplaceable stuff.

She wanted the blue-and-yellow log cabin quilt that Nana had worked so hard and so long to make for Laura's eighteenth birthday. She wanted Nana's sachet-scented linen hankies with the tatted edges and her mother's cross-stitched pillowcases. She wanted all the treasured photographs of her mother and Nana, even the mutilated pictures where her father had been less than artfully snipped out.

She wanted the daisy that Billy Dean had given her at summer camp when she was ten, the one that she had pressed between the pages of her favorite Nancy Drew book. Her diary from seventh grade. Her report cards. The shoebox with every birthday card she'd ever gotten in her life. Right now she even wanted the stupid philodendron that she'd half killed last year and then nursed back to life.

But they were all gone now. Ashes. Everything.

Laura was barely aware that Sam had stopped the truck until he opened the passenger door for her.

"Here we are," he said.

She reached into the back seat for the paper bag that held the blue velvet dress, a change of underwear, rhinestone-studded and tar-streaked stiletto heels, a hairbrush and a toothbrush—the sad sum of her worldly goods.

"I feel like a refugee," she muttered, sounding as pitiful as she felt, allowing Sam to grasp her elbow to help her out of the truck.

When he didn't let go of her arm immediately, Laura felt the beguiling warmth that even his most casual touch could generate. Oh, no. Not that. She gently pulled away. Coming back here hadn't been a good idea. Grateful as she was for Sam's help, she didn't want him helping her right into bed again.

"Sam," she said softly, but firmly, "please, don't."

He blinked. "What'd I do?" His expression was

so innocent, so sincerely bewildered that Laura almost laughed.

"You were touching me," she said.

"I was not," he protested.

"Yes, you were. On my arm."

"That? That wasn't *touching* touching. I wasn't trying…"

Laura sighed. "Well, it felt like *touching* touching to me. Just don't, Sam. Okay?"

Sam sighed roughly and raked his fingers through his hair. Laura swore she saw a flush of color stain his cheeks, and she wasn't sure whether it came from embarrassment or anger.

"It won't happen again," he said, splaying his hand over his heart. "I promise, Laura." Then he held up two fingers. "Scout's honor."

"You're not a Scout," Laura said, narrowing her eyes.

He grinned. "Well, I'll join up, then."

That, Laura thought, would surely set a few den mothers' hearts aflutter, if not wildly aflame.

Sam did his best to keep his distance from Laura the rest of the day, figuring he couldn't touch her if he wasn't within three feet of her. During lunch and dinner, he felt relatively safe with the wide expanse of the kitchen table between them.

Laura, in an effort not to be an imposition, had prepared their lunch. Sam hadn't had a peanut butter and jelly sandwich accompanied by carrot sticks since third or fourth grade. For dinner, he whipped up some comfort food, hoping it would help to ease the pain of her loss.

It was over dinner that she finally brought up the subject of the Hammer. About time, Sam thought.

"So," she asked between bites of meat loaf, mashed potatoes and peas, "How do you know Art Hammerman?"

"I don't really know him all that well. I did some work for him a year or so ago."

She looked surprised. "The Hammer hired a private eye? With all the muscle he keeps on his payroll? Why?"

"I guess he didn't want the boys on the payroll to know that he was having a few marital problems."

"Ah. Well, you must have taken care of those since I heard he got a divorce last winter."

Sam decided to ignore the sarcastic tilt of the eyebrow above the ever-changing purple-and-green shiner.

"Tell me about Artie," he said, putting down his fork and leaning back while he watched Laura swallow a bite of partially chewed meat loaf then quickly reach for her water glass. She took a long and very thoughtful drink. Thoughtful as in scrambling mentally to come up with a story, any story at all that he might actually believe. He could practically hear the frantic whirl of activity inside her pretty head.

"Artie," she said at last, accompanying her words with a soft cluck of her tongue and a slight lift of her shoulders. "I guess you've figured it out, huh?"

Sam nodded, keeping the skeptical expression on his face even as he let out a silent sigh of relief. He realized all of a sudden that he'd been holding his breath in anticipation of Laura's reply. It was one thing to understand why she had lied before. That was for survival. It made sense. But if she lied to him now, he knew his feelings for her—whatever they were—would diminish.

"I'm sorry I lied, Sam," she said, her gaze holding steady on his. "It's just that I was afraid you wouldn't help me if I told you the truth."

"It wouldn't have made any difference. I would've helped you anyway. The minute you walked into my office, I..." He stopped speaking the moment he realized that his hand, almost of its own accord, was about to reach out to touch the bruise beneath her eye.

"You what?" she asked, cocking her head to one side, locking her blue eyes on him, apparently enjoying her ability to make him squirm.

"I, uh... The minute you walked into my office, I said to myself 'Now there's somebody who could use a little help.'"

"You did not." She gave a little laugh. "You said to yourself 'What's this hooker doing so far away from her street corner?'"

"It's good to hear you laugh, Laura," he said softly, almost having to sit on his hands now to keep from touching her.

But as soon as he said it, all the merriment disappeared from her face and her eyes glistened with tears.

"For a second," she said, swiping at one wet eye, "I almost forgot that those hooker clothes are the only things I have left. Thanks to Artie. I don't suppose there's any way they'll ever prove he did it."

Sam only shrugged. He still didn't want to tell her about the lightning, thinking it would frighten her more than she already was. He wasn't lying, exactly, he told himself.

Merely diverting the truth.

"Arson's tricky," he mumbled, rising to clear the table of their empty dishes.

But Laura was on her feet instantly, pulling the plate from his hand. "Let me do this, Sam. You go on. Go do whatever you usually do in the evenings. Play the piano or something."

"You sure?"

"I'm sure. It's about the only way I can pay you back right now."

"Okay. I'll be downstairs, Laura. Give a shout if you need me."

He headed down the stairs. Playing the piano was probably a good idea. If nothing else, it would occupy his wayward hands.

Instead of just rinsing the dishes and stacking them in the dishwasher, Laura filled the sink with hot, soapy water, then diligently, almost lovingly scrubbed the plates and glasses and silverware. She'd never considered it a chore to do the dishes, even when she was young. It was pleasant to stand at the sink, gazing out the window, feeling the steam rise to her face, letting the water warm her hands.

Right now, in her homeless state, it felt good, even reassuring, just to touch each object. The plates with their antiquated blue-and-white pattern of Chinese bridges and willow trees and men porting buckets of water on poles across their shoulders. The plain, tall glasses and the short ones with Daffy Duck and Tweety Bird, all of them getting squeaky clean under her fingers, while Sam's lovely music filtered up through the floorboards.

He was good, she thought, and then she started

thinking how her mother had always wanted a piano. If she had one, though, she would have willed it to Laura, and then it would have wound up as toast, along with everything else in her apartment.

She started missing her stuff again, desperately, so before she scraped her plate into the trash can, she popped the last bit of Sam's comforting meat loaf in her mouth. Still chewing luxuriously when the phone rang, Laura waited a moment to see if Sam had heard it, then grabbed a towel, dried her hands, and answered it as clearly as anyone could with a mouth full of meat loaf.

After the man on the other end of the line asked to speak to Sam, she swallowed and called out to him, but he still didn't hear her. She had to go halfway down the stairs and yell to be heard over the loud chords he was playing.

"Sorry. I didn't hear it," he said, trotting up the stairs behind her. "Who's on the phone?"

"I have no idea," she said, handing him the receiver and returning to the sink to finish up the meat loaf pan.

While she scrubbed and dug the dishrag into every corner, she couldn't help but overhear Sam's end of the conversation. Although it was mostly a string of *uh-huhs* and *okays,* his tone struck Laura as guarded, even slightly suspicious. But then she probably shouldn't be surprised. She supposed private investigators got more than their share of weird phone calls.

She had begun to dry the plates and put them away when Sam finally hung up.

"Who was that?" she asked more out of politeness than curiosity.

"You didn't recognize the voice?"

"No." She put the last plate in the cabinet, closed the door and turned toward him. "Should I have?"

"Probably. That was your pal, Artie."

"What?"

Her heart vaulted into her throat. She felt a little dizzy. "I don't understand, Sam. Why...why would Artie be calling here? Calling you?"

He lowered himself into a chair at the table and sat staring into space for a moment, drumming his fingers while he shook his head.

"Sam," Laura pressed. "Why is he calling here? How did he get your number?"

His gaze finally focused on her. "From his father. It seems the love of Artie's life has turned up missing. He wants to hire a private eye to find her."

Laura almost laughed. A little strangling sound rolled in the depths of her throat. This couldn't be happening. It was just too bizarre. "Well, you told him no, didn't you? You told him that you couldn't do it, right?"

He shook his head. "No. I took the job."

She felt her eyes nearly pop out of their sockets and her jaw come unhinged. "You took the job!"

He nodded now. "Yeah. I told him I'd find you for him."

Laura could hardly breathe. She could hardly speak. "Why?" she croaked.

A sly grin worked its way across Sam's lips and the crinkles at the corners of his eyes deepened when he said, "I took the job so our friend Artie doesn't call the next P.I. on his list."

Chapter 9

Sam rowed five hard miles that night after Laura
went up to bed. In the basement, inside his head, the
imaginary weather over the North Atlantic was over-
cast and the visibility extremely low. In other words,
Sam was in a fog and didn't have a clue what was
going to happen next.

One thing he knew for certain was that it was
pretty unethical, agreeing to do a job that he had no
intention of carrying out. But what other choice did
he have? There was no way in the world he was
going to leave Art Hammerman, Jr., free to call another investigator and put the guy on Laura's trail.

What he was doing might even be illegal, border-
ing on fraud, he guessed, because to do a convincing
job, Sam was going to have to take Artie's money
and give him regular, if bogus, progress reports.

He'd had a hell of a time convincing Laura that

he wasn't actually going over to the other side, that he had no intention of handing her over to the enemy.

"You're my client, Laura, for God's sake," he'd told her.

"But I'm not officially your client anymore," she'd said. "And even if I were, I can't pay you, Sam."

"Then, I'm helping you as a friend."

"But we're not friends," she'd said.

He hadn't known how to respond to that.

Because Laura was absolutely right. They weren't friends, not in the sense that they shared memories or knew each other's hopes and dreams. This wasn't what he wanted. He had his own private memories. He didn't want to share anybody's hopes and dreams. That implied a future, and all he wanted was his past. He sure as hell hadn't been looking for a friend or a bedmate when Laura had picked him out of the Yellow Pages and strolled into his office in her impossibly high heels.

He didn't know what they were. But he knew what he didn't want them to be, which was lovers of any kind. The promises he'd made to Jenny were real. The fact that she was dead didn't change anything as far as he was concerned. He belonged to Jenny. Period. He always had, and he always would.

He slowed the pace of his rowing, bringing the imaginary wind down to a single knot and putting it at his back. His thoughts, however, kept racing ahead.

All he and Laura had in common was sex. A couple of hot, volatile moments. Nothing else. Maybe they were the proverbial opposites who were irresistibly attracted to each other. Sam had never experi-

enced anything like it before, but that could explain
the physical magnetism every time they touched.
Even when they didn't touch, the pull was still there.

Wanting something he didn't want. Wanting
someone he didn't want. He couldn't understand it.
Even so, he ought to be able to control it easily
enough. He'd simply keep his distance.

The rest of the attraction, he decided, was just his
innate protective nature. He was drawn to people in
trouble. He was still the kid on the playground, chas-
ing away bullies, picking up fallen lollipops and
brushing them off and handing them back to little
girls with wet eyes and skinned knees.

For a second he wondered what Laura had looked
like when she was in kindergarten, wondered where
she had hidden during storms and who, if anyone,
had held her and whispered it was all right.

Then he forced himself to stop wondering.

Don't wonder.

Don't touch her.

Don't even think about her.

Think about Jenny instead.

"Jenny. God, I miss you, Jen. I just don't know
how to be without you."

The next morning Laura tiptoed down the stairs,
not wanting to disturb Sam. His bedroom door was
closed, but even so she could hear the faint snoring
that signaled solid sleep.

She wished she could have said the same for herself, doubting that she'd had even an hour of sleep
the night before. Every time she closed her eyes, her
brain would begin to catalog possessions she had
lost, then she'd have to sit up, reach for the tissue

box on the nightstand, dry her eyes and blow her nose. By morning, with the tissue box nearly empty and hardly any tears left, Laura decided to make a concerted effort to snap out of it and to cheer the hell up.

One way to get her mind off her troubles, she concluded, was to fix a fabulous breakfast for Sam. How hard could an omelette be, after all? Eggs weren't so scary. Neither was cheese. But when she opened the refrigerator and found herself standing on one foot and then the other, staring stupidly at packages of Parmesan, Gruyère, Fontina and feta, Laura suddenly remembered why she always ate the same brand of cold cereal in the mornings. Who could make these decisions so early in the day? Jeez. Who even wanted to?

She poured a glass of orange juice and got the coffeemaker going, enjoying its busy gurgling while she listened for sounds of life upstairs. After a few minutes, there was a creak in a floorboard overhead, followed shortly by faint shower noises. Sam was up!

Why that made her smile and caused her heart to beat a little faster, Laura couldn't have said. She'd spent half the night clutching her pillow to her face, trying to silence her sobs so Sam wouldn't feel obliged to comfort her. If they were indeed friends, as he had said, then she intended for them to stay that way. Just friends. Nothing more.

The shower was still running upstairs, and it was easy to picture Sam's big hands plying a bar of soap into a lather, the white foam working into the wet fur on his chest, then the suds streaming down his corded abdomen and strong calves to disappear in a swirl down the drain.

What was she thinking?

Delicious as it was, Laura forced the image from her brain. Friends, after all, didn't conjure up images of each other in the shower. Did they? Friends met for lunch and dinner. They traded gossip and books. They gave each other birthday presents and good advice. But they kept their clothes on all the while and maintained a seemly, friendly distance.

She retrieved a cup from the cabinet and was pouring herself some of the freshly brewed coffee when there was a knock on the back door. She stared at the door a moment, remembering that the last time somebody had knocked she'd been wearing Sam's shirt and had gotten the hairy eyeball from Janey Sayles. This time she was at least clothed, although she couldn't vouch for the fragrance of her jeans and T-shirt on their second day of wear.

She opened the door only slightly warily, but instead of Janey with a sour look on her face, there was a uniformed man with a great big grin.

"Morning, ma'am," he said.

"Hi," Laura said, eyeing the gleaming badge on the breast pocket of his brown shirt. "You're with the county sheriff's department. Is something wrong?"

"Oh, no. Nothing's wrong. I just stopped by to have a little talk with Sam." He leaned to his left and peered over her shoulder into the kitchen. "He up yet?"

"Well, he's..."

"He's up."

Sam's voice sounded behind her. Laura turned to see his showered, slicked-back hair and freshly shaven face. He was dressed in his usual navy polo shirt and softly faded jeans, and as he came closer, the fragrance of soap and shaving cream was so luscious, so incredibly beguiling that Laura had to fight off her earlier sudsy and overly familiar visions.

"Come on in. Charlie," he said, "this is my friend, Laura McNeal. Laura, this is Charlie Travis."

Friend. There was that word again, Laura thought.

"Oh, I don't want to bother you, Sam." Officer Travis's gaze bounced meaningfully from Sam to Laura and back. "Actually, I stopped to ask if you noticed anything suspicious around here last night. We got a couple calls about a possible prowler in the area."

"A prowler!" Laura gasped.

"It was probably nothing, ma'am." He gave her a quick smile meant to be reassuring before he said to Sam, "We sent out a patrol car, but Donovan didn't see anything except for a coyote going through a spilled trash can."

Laura gasped again, louder. "A coyote! Oh, my God."

Officer Travis's smile this time seemed a little more condescending than reassuring. "They're a lot more afraid of you, ma'am, than you are of them."

"That's what you think," Laura said.

Sam chuckled. "Well, then, it'd probably be a good idea for you to wait inside while I go out and talk some more to Charlie."

He moved past her, still smelling divine in a friendly sort of way, and pushed open the screen door.

Laura drank a second cup of coffee while the two of them conversed on the back porch. She tried to eavesdrop, but found their low tones impossible to decipher. She tried to decide which was worse, a prowler or a coyote, and finally decided on the prowler, thinking that Artie could disguise himself as one of those, but being so squat and muscle-bound, he could never in a million years pass for a coyote.

When Sam came back in, he looked worried. His forehead was furrowed and the set of his mouth was pretty grim.

"What's the verdict?" she asked. "Prowler or coyote?"

"Coyote," he said, grinning a bit as he watched her shiver.

"Aren't they dangerous?"

He shook his head. "Not really. They're more—"

"I know. I know." Laura rolled her eyes. "More afraid of me than I am of them. Well, if that's true, there must be some terrified coyotes running around out there."

"It's nothing to worry about," he said as he poured a cup of coffee, then proceeded to shovel an ungodly amount of sugar into it. "Charlie stops by on some lame excuse every couple of weeks to try to get me to run for county sheriff again. He's not too thrilled with my replacement."

"You were the sheriff?" she asked, trying to imagine him in a brown shirt similar to Charlie's, only more trim and tailored. "I didn't know that, Sam. Why did you quit?"

"I stopped being good at it."

The answer, accompanied by a shrug, was casual enough, but Laura saw something flicker deep in Sam's eyes when he spoke. She'd never seen him look quite so sad. Poor Sam. Laura wondered if quitting his job as sheriff had something to do with his dead fiancée, but she didn't want to pursue a subject that seemed to cause him so much pain.

"I think you're good at everything," she said.

That sad smile turned ineffably sweet. Laura wondered if he thought she was including lovemaking in the everything he was good at. But if that had been the case, she would have said great.

"I'm not good at much," she added almost as an afterthought, then immediately regretted her candor. It made her sound so pitiful. "I mean, I can't cook or play the piano."

"You could if you tried. Hell, anybody can follow a recipe or read notes on a page, Laura."

"Almost anybody," she corrected. "The last time I tried to cook, the men from the fire department suggested I'd be better off eating out."

"You have to cook," he said, taking a sip of his sugar-laden brew.

"No, I don't."

"What are you going to do when you get married and have a family?"

She laughed. "That's easy. I'm not going to *get* married and have a family."

"Sure you are."

"No," she said a bit more firmly, "I'm not."

Sam was looking at her as if she were a lunatic instead of a very rational person who had long ago concluded that her heart couldn't be broken if she didn't play the game, that a man couldn't leave her if she never invited him to stay.

"Are you?" she asked him.

"Am I what?"

"Going to get married and have a family?"

Now he looked at her as if she were a lunatic whose hair was on fire. "Well, no, *I'm* not, but that's completely different. You're a young, beautiful woman, Laura, with your whole life ahead of you."

"Well, what are you, Sam? A doddering old man with his life behind him?"

Instead of laughing at her question and dismissing it, he actually seemed to be seriously considering it while he sipped his coffee and worked his forehead into worried lines. For the first time since she'd met him, Laura got the impression that Sam Zachary hadn't the slightest idea that he was a hunk. He was back in Clark Kent mode at the moment, oblivious of his alter ego.

"I'm just pretty set in my ways," he finally said.

"Ah. The old confirmed-bachelor routine."

"Something like that." He looked at his watch. "It's getting late. I've got a meeting in town. Want me to drop you off someplace to shop for a while?"

"Shop?"

His gaze warmed significantly as it took her in from head to toe. "Unless you intend to wear those jeans and that T-shirt the rest of your life."

"Oh. I guess I do need to get a few things, don't I?" She sighed, trying to ward off feelings of sadness and loss, trying to generate a bit of enthusiasm at the prospect of a whole new wardrobe. "Let me run upstairs and get my checkbook."

"Take your time."

She started to leave, then turned back. "This meeting of yours? It wouldn't happen to be with a new client named Artie, would it?"

He nodded. "It'll be okay. Trust me."

"Famous last words," she muttered. But in spite of all her fears, Laura was beginning to think she did.

"Cash is okay, right?"

Even as he asked, Art Hammerman, Jr., was slowly peeling five hundreds from a wad of bills he'd pulled from the pocket of his loose, pleated pants. For some reason Sam couldn't fathom, the kid dressed like somebody trying out for a part in *Guys and Dolls*.

"Cash is fine," Sam said, glancing around at what young Artie referred to as his office, which in reality was a storage room tucked in a far corner of the spacious Hammerman Building. It was probably the Hammer's way of keeping his aggressive son on a very short leash.

"My father says you do good work," Artie said, handing the bills across the empty expanse of his desktop.

"I appreciate that. Thanks." He jammed the money in his pocket, ignoring his feelings of guilt and apprehensions about losing his P.I. license. "Now, what can I do for you?"

"There's this girl..."

For the next twenty minutes or so, Sam sat expressionless while young Artie Hammerman attempted to describe Laura McNeal, his feelings for her, and his eagerness to find her.

As he listened, Sam found himself silently editing the kid's descriptions. The face that Artie described as *real cute,* Sam pictured as beautiful beyond belief. The eyes that Artie saw as *kinda blue, maybe gray,* Sam saw as cornflowers speckled with bits of golden pollen. He couldn't even allow himself to think about the bruise, knowing he'd be tempted to do the same to the perpetrator.

She wasn't *short*. Jenny had been short, but Laura's head, when he held her, fit beneath his chin as if she'd been custom-designed for him. And she wasn't *on the skinny side*. She was just right, and perfectly fleshed out from her trim calves to her soft, fragrant neck. Her breasts. Ah, God. Her breasts were...

"So, anyway, Zachary, this chick's really hot," Artie said in summation. "And I want her back."

Over my dead body, bozo. "I'll see what I can do."

"Keep me posted, will you?"

"Oh, yeah."

Sam left Artie with the impression that he was the strong and silent type, rather than the unethical and lying type, and while he was driving to the mall where he had dropped off Laura earlier, he seriously considered stopping by his office, cleaning it out, and closing it up for good.

What a lousy way to make a living. He never felt he actually helped anybody, but only increased their misery.

I'm sorry. Your birth mother died three years ago.

I'm sorry. Here are the photographs of your wife and her seventeen-year-old lover.

Sorry, ma'am, but your husband hasn't been playing pinochle on Tuesday nights all these years.

He'd enjoyed his years in the military, but it was the job as sheriff that he'd truly loved. He felt helpful, whether it was putting up a roadblock after a bank robbery or deploying his limited personnel for a murder investigation or just generally keeping watch over the sixteen thousand souls in his county.

Then Jenny had died and he couldn't even keep watch over himself for a while. When she skidded off the road, so had he. The marriage he'd looked forward to would never happen. Or the children.

As he turned into the mall parking lot, his mind veered, as well, from Jenny to Laura. Why the hell was the woman so determined never to marry and have kids? In his experience, all women wanted families. Didn't they?

Jenny had wanted that even though she'd postponed it until it was too late. Janey Sayles had wanted a child so badly that she'd hopscotched over the notion of marriage in order to have Samantha all to herself. One of his female deputies had taken a leave of absence to do the same.

Even though he'd had his chance and lost it, Sam still believed that marriage and family were essential to happiness. Just because he was no longer a candidate for happiness, didn't mean that everyone else shouldn't be.

He braked for a young woman pushing a stroller while pulling another child along by the hand. She resembled Laura, even though she wasn't half so lithe or lovely. What a waste, he thought, for those shapely genes not to be passed on, if only to beautify the world.

Sam parked, then headed for the mall's front entrance, hoping he wouldn't have to play detective and scope out three-dozen stores before he found her. He figured her for a boutique and kiosk shopper, flitting from one concession to another, rather than one who patronized sensible, sell-all department stores. Still fifty yards from the main doors, his heart kicked in an extra beat when he saw her just outside the entrance, perched on a huge cement flower pot, her face turned up toward the noon sky like a pretty sunflower.

A smile ignited on his face and he lifted a hand to wave just as a baseball-capped kid on roller blades shot past Laura, snatching her little beaded purse.

"Hold it!" Sam shouted out, then sprinted after the kid who was already threading his way across the parking lot, weaving in and out of cars at an amazing clip, probably headed for the Wilson Boulevard exit, hoping to lose himself in lunchtime traffic.

Sam cut through a gaggle of teenage girls, vaulted over the hood of a Jeep, beat the kid to the exit by two seconds, then grabbed back the purse just as the little felon flew past. Damn. If he'd had his Reebok trainers on, he would have pursued the kid and dragged his sorry ass into mall security, but wearing his leather-soled loafers, he already considered himself pretty lucky not to have broken his neck.

"You rotten creep!" Laura appeared at Sam's elbow, her face flushed from her own race across the parking lot, her fist shaking in the direction of the disappearing roller blader.

Sam dragged in a few deep breaths. "Here." He slapped the little beaded bag in Laura's hand. "Hang onto it now, will you? I'm not as fast as I used to be."

"Fast enough," she said, drawing the bag's strap up her arm and securing it over her shoulder. "Thank you, Sam."

She smiled up at him, but her lips wavered and her pretty face sort of pruned up when she said, "I'd hate to lose this, too. It's all I've got left of my grandmother.''

"You're welcome." He refrained from adding "That's what friends are for" because it sounded way too sappy and her *friend* was sorely tempted to kiss those quivering lips just then. "Are you all done shopping?"

She nodded.

"Good. Let's go home." He looped his arm around her shoulder. "Home where the only bad guys are spiders and coyotes."

Sam was negotiating traffic, but he was still able to glance at the few meager shopping bags Laura had tossed into the back seat. "Is that all you bought?" he asked.

She wasn't sure whether his frown was from irritation with her or simply from bright sunlight reflecting off the chrome on the car ahead of them.

"I tried. I really did. Nothing appealed to me."

"You've got to have clothes," he said.

Laura let out a soft little sigh of disgust. "Maybe I should join a nudist colony. That would solve my homelessness and my wardrobe problem in one fell swoop."

He chuckled, unaware that she was almost serious.

She had drifted around the mall for an hour and a half, fingering fabrics, rarely taking an item off the rack for closer inspection. If the color was right, the style was wrong. If the style had even minor appeal, there were major problems with its price. In the end, she'd plucked two bras and half a dozen pairs of panties from a sale bin, added a pair of jeans and a couple tops, then called it a day.

"How'd it go with Artie?" she asked, hoping Sam's morning had been better than her own.

"Okay."

"I take it you're on his payroll, then?"

"Yep." He slanted a grin in her direction. "Don't tell anybody in the Better Business Bureau, will you?"

"Not as long as you don't tell rotten Artie where I am." She tried to laugh, but it came out as a pitiful groan. "Oh, Sam. What am I going to do?"

"We'll figure something out," he said.

By the time they got home, however, they hadn't figured out anything except what to have for lunch. While Sam's head and shoulders all but disappeared inside the refrigerator, Laura took her packages upstairs. She had barely put her foot on the first step when she smelled something burning. The odor was unpleasant, acrid, like burning plastic.

She shouted for Sam as she raced up the stairs. Not seeing any smoke, she followed her nose and headed for the bathroom where it only took a second to locate the source of the foul smell. An electric curling iron was melting its way through the Formica countertop of the vanity.

For a panicky second, Laura didn't know what to do. Unplug it? Throw water on it? What?

Then Sam sort of lifted her out of his way, plucked the cord from the wall switch, and poured a glass of water on the countertop. The curling iron sizzled and sent up a thin shaft of gray smoke.

They both stood there a moment just looking at it, then Sam wrenched open the window.

"You must've forgotten to turn it off this morning,'' he said in a voice that betrayed a good deal of irritation.

Laura blinked at the black melted mess. Under the plastic, the vanity's wooden frame was charred. My God, if they hadn't returned when they had...

"I didn't..." She was sure she had unplugged the appliance after she'd used it this morning. She distinctly remembered scowling in the mirror at the limp curls it had produced, then pulling the plug out, wrapping the cord around the handle and replacing the curler in the little closet next to the tub.

Or was that yesterday?

"I'm sure I unplugged it, Sam," she said, despite the niggling doubt.

He picked the appliance up, using a washcloth on the hot handle, and held it for a minute like some dead thing, dangling from his hand above the wreckage of the countertop.

"Oh, Sam. I'm so sorry."

"Just be more careful, will you?" he said, shouldering past her, muttering under his breath all the way down the stairs.

In the kitchen, Sam dropped the curling gizmo in the trash can. It wasn't such a terrible mistake, he thought, even though the consequences could have been disastrous. A brief, disturbing image of his house in smoking ruins, similar to Laura's apartment, flashed through his brain. For a second he nearly forgot that she wasn't to blame for that catastrophe.

He slapped a few pieces of bacon into a pan and turned up the flame beneath it. Maybe it was a blessing that Laura had given up cooking, he thought. She couldn't clean without bringing down mirrors. She couldn't shop, apparently, without getting her purse snatched. Trouble seemed to follow her like her very own shadow.

"Can I help?"

Hearing her voice behind him, Sam let his eyes sink closed. Surely there was something this woman could do well other than turn his bloodstream to liquid fire every time she came near him? He reached for the white plastic colander.

"Think you can battle your way through the spiders and grasshoppers again for a couple tomatoes and some lettuce? I'm making us BLTs."

"Oh. Sure. No problem."

She took the colander from him, marched to the door, and stood there surveying the backyard as if she suspected a sniper in every tree and a coyote behind every bush.

"Just yell if you need me," Sam said encouragingly.

"Right." She sighed. "What was it you wanted? Lettuce?"

"And tomatoes. You know. Those red things. Don't pick the green ones. They're not ripe yet."

"Got it." She did one more quick surveillance of the battlefield and then charged forth.

Sam was slicing whole wheat bread when she called him.

"I think you ought to come out here, Sam. It's the tomatoes. Something's not right."

He turned down the heat under the frying pan. Laura's idea of something not right with the tomatoes was probably the absence of plastic trays and shrink-wrap and UPC codes. She was down on her knees, peering into the greenery when he got there. And what was not right about the tomatoes was instantly and sickeningly clear. The plants, in their entirety, had been ripped from the ground.

All he could do was stare for a minute in mute disbelief before he was able to shout, "What did you do, for chrissake? You're supposed to pick the tomatoes, not the whole goddamned plant."

"I didn't!"

He bent to pick up one of the plants, its top heavily laden with green fruit and its exposed roots matted with soil. He almost thought he'd cry. "What were you thinking, Laura?"

"I didn't *do* this, Sam," she said, getting to her feet, furiously brushing bits of leaf and grass from her knees. "Give me a break. I mean, even I know enough to know you don't rip a whole tomato plant from the ground."

He was reaching deeper into the foliage, checking to see if any plants were still viable, but not a single one of the six lush bushes had been spared. "I just don't understand this," he said.

"Well, um… Do coyotes attack tomatoes?"

He aimed a scorching glare over his shoulder, causing Laura to murmur sheepishly, "Okay. I guess not."

"Hand me the colander, will you? I'll salvage what I can."

"Here. Let me help."

"No." He brushed away her fluttering hand and at the same time felt like a lout for blaming her when he knew it wasn't her fault. "I'll do it," he said, deliberately softening his tone. "Why don't you just go on in the house."

After Laura walked away, Sam closed his eyes a

minute. Somebody was sending a message. That was clear enough. But damned if he knew what that message was, or—more importantly—who it was for.

He heaped the white plastic bowl with ripe and nearly ripe tomatoes, leaving dozens of green ones to die, then followed Laura into the house.

Chapter 10

"I know who did it," Laura said before she popped the final, luscious, gooey bite of the world's greatest BLT into her mouth, and tried hard not to moan with pleasure while she chewed.

Across the table, Sam's lips slid into a distinct sneer while one of his eyebrows crooked upward. He'd been so quiet and glum all during lunch, presumably mourning his tomatoes, that Laura almost didn't mind the current, healthy display of skepticism on his face.

"Really," she added for emphasis. "I know who did it."

"Right," he said with a pronounced snort.

"It's obvious, Sam."

"Oh, yeah? Well, maybe you should apply for a P.I. license, Laura, if these things come so easily to you. I could sublease my office to you since I'm hardly using it anyway."

"Don't be sarcastic."

"I wasn't, actually."

She dabbed a bit of mayonnaise from the corner of her mouth, then folded her napkin into a perfect little square and nudged it under her empty plate. How could he not want to know her theory?

"Okay. Well, just forget I mentioned it." Crossing her arms, she leaned back. Her smile, she hoped, wasn't too terribly smug. Just smug enough and hopefully infectious enough to make Zachary, S. U. sit there and itch with curiosity.

"All right," he said finally. "I know you're dying to tell me, so go ahead. Who was it?"

"Pardon me?" She leaned forward, lofting her brows, widening her eyes innocently, cupping a hand to her ear as if she hadn't quite heard him. "What did you say?"

"You heard me."

"Oh. Who was it?" Laura tried not to laugh. "Is that what you asked?"

He simply cocked his head, waiting, those gorgeous brown eyes of his glittering while they locked tightly on hers.

"You really want to know?" She cocked her head at the same angle and batted her eyelashes some more. She wished she had a fan to flit in front of her face while she grinned behind it.

"I really want to know," he said. "Lay it on me, Sherlock."

"Actually, Watson, my dear, it's elementary. The culprit is your pal, Janey."

Sam flinched. He looked as if she had just reached across the table to slap him. The light in his eyes shut down as his entire face darkened.

"Okay. That's enough," he said, shoving back his chair, standing, snatching up his plate. "You're way out of line, Laura. *Way* out of line."

Laura was stunned. She thought her theory might surprise him, or maybe even amuse him, but she never in a million years expected it to make him angry. Angry? God, he was furious. A vein was visibly throbbing at his temple, and his mouth was battened down so tightly that his lips were almost white. The air in the kitchen fairly crackled as he stalked toward the sink.

"Well, wait a minute, Sam," she sputtered. "I mean, it's just a theory, but think about it. Janey's…"

"That's enough, Laura."

"It's just that…"

"Stop!"

His plate shattered in the sink. He turned with his hands clenched at his sides in an obvious, terrifying effort at control. When he spoke, his voice was level, but ominously low. "Not one more word about Janey. I mean that, Laura. Not one more word. Do you understand?"

No, she really didn't understand at all, but she nodded anyway. She even bit her lower lip to guarantee her own silence. Sam looked capable of killing somebody at the moment. Her!

"Laura," he said, then stopped to drag in a long breath and let it out slowly, as if he were counting to ten. No, he stood there so long it was more as if he were counting to ten thousand. When he spoke again, his eyes were hard as bullets and his voice was even lower and lethally cold.

"This is none of your business, Laura. You

walked into my office a few days ago. Don't...do *not* for one second confuse that with walking into my life.''

The chill that shot through her entire body was painful, almost numbing. It left her with barely enough strength to rise from her chair, to face him squarely, and to say, ''It was easy to walk in, Sam. But, trust me, it's going to be even easier to walk out.''

Laura slammed the front door behind her, stomped down the porch steps, and headed for the road, a shopping bag clenched in each fist. The one advantage in being a refugee was a minimum of baggage, and the one advantage in being blazingly, blindingly angry was that she wasn't the least bit worried about where she was going. Away was good enough at the moment.

Away was *great*.

Laura picked up her pace. At the end of the short stretch of gravel road, she paused for a second, sorely tempted to turn around for one last glimpse of the lovely white clapboard house, all snug within its wraparound porch and rose bushes, but she was afraid that Sam would be standing there and he was the one person she never wanted to see again in her life. So, instead of taking a last look back at the house, she glanced up through the trees at the afternoon sky.

Uh-oh.

When had the clouds begun to turn such a horrible, sickening shade of gray? It had been sunny all morning. In fact, there hadn't even been any clouds. Now they were scudding across the sky, joining together to form bigger, denser, more threatening shapes, obliterating the sun. The wind seemed to be picking up, too. Just then a sudden gust brutally twisted the trees above her, bringing leaves and twigs down on her head.

This was not good.

This was very, very bad.

Laura's heart started to pound, but even so she could hear the tiny voice at the back of her brain. *Go back,* it urged her.

"No way."

She gripped her shopping bags tighter and walked faster, turning right onto the canopied blacktop that would eventually lead to the highway.

Go back to Sam's? Never in a million years. Not after he had turned on her so viciously. Her friend! What a joke! How could he be so deliberately cruel, telling her she'd walked into his office, not his life?

Taking Janey to the emergency room in the dead of the night and driving through a hurricane to do it apparently was nothing to him, but let Laura make one teensy remark that rubbed him the wrong way and *Bam!* He'd let her have it with both barrels, right between the eyes.

Walk back into his life? Not on *her* life. Not if she lived to be a thousand years old. Not ever.

She walked faster, away, every now and then looking up and squinting through the trees at the ever-darkening sky.

Go back? Go to hell, Sam Zachary. She'd rather get fried by lightning.

"Just kidding," she muttered under her breath.

In the pasture to her left, Laura could see cows moving together, closing ranks in a tight circle of black and white, while the wind whipped through the surrounding grasses. Birds leapt from the fence posts along the side of the road, then seemed to be carried away on the wind rather than flying on their own.

Not good. Not good. Oh, God, this wasn't good. She didn't mean it about the lightning, really.

Go back.

"No way."

Then the rain came. Sideways. Slashing at Laura's face and arms. Soaking her hair and clothes. Still, it was only rain. Rain was harmless enough. It was just vertical water. At least there wasn't any...

Thunder shook the ground beneath her feet, reverberating up through Laura's whole body. Her eyes nearly popped out of her head as she looked frantically around for shelter and found nothing but trees and fence posts. There wasn't even a ditch in which to flatten herself.

A scream was clawing its way up her throat just as the truck pulled up beside her and the passenger door swung open.

"Get in."

Sam pulled to the side of the road, cut the wipers and the engine, then flicked on the hazard lights. The wind was blowing hard enough to punish the two thousand pound Blazer, and the rain cascaded in a thick, gray sheet down the windshield. The lightning was close and fierce.

"Hell of a storm," he said, half turning, leaning his back against the door, with one arm draped over the steering wheel, the other over the seat back.

Laura nodded. Her wet hair flung beads of water across the dash. She was shaking so hard her bones were nearly rattling in her skin. After what he'd said to her, though, he'd be surprised if she accepted his comfort.

"I've got a hug I'm not using," he said softly. "You need one?"

She shook her head vehemently, sending forth another spray of water, just before a resonant clap of thunder sent her scrambling across the center console and into his ready arms.

"I hate this. I hate this. I hate this," she muttered into the front of his shirt.

"I know. It'll be over soon."

Sam sat there, holding Laura, trying to absorb her shivers and her fears, trying not to notice how good it felt to have her in his arms again. Not that he deserved feeling good after lashing out at her the way he had a little while ago. Hell, he suspected Janey, too. He just didn't want to deal with it, and so he'd behaved like an insensitive clod.

He pressed his cheek against Laura's wet, fragrant hair, closed his eyes, and selfishly hoped the storm would go on for at least another hour.

It didn't. The rain slackened and the fierce winds blew themselves out in a mere ten minutes, and Laura made a strangled little sound as she began to push herself away from him. But Sam didn't let her go. He held her even closer against him.

"I'm sorry," he said, "I shouldn't have said what I did. You know, that bit about you walking into my office but not my life. I didn't mean it."

She went completely still within the circle of his arms, and Sam didn't know if that meant she accepted his apology without further explanation or if she was merely gathering her strength, ticking like a silent time bomb prior to exploding.

All he knew was that he didn't want to let her go. This woman had done more than merely walk into his life. She had altered his lone existence completely, changed it for the better somehow, irrevocably, only he didn't know how to explain it to her much less to himself.

"What *did* you mean, then?" Her words were muffled in his shirtfront, warm against his chest.

Sam sighed, smoothing his hand along her damp upper arm. "Damned if I know," he said. "Other than I don't want you to go. I don't know any other way to say it, Laura."

"Try," she said, apparently unwilling to let him off the hook.

He closed his eyes. "I'm not good at this," he said, struggling to find the words that would help her understand what he hardly understood himself. Was he in love? Or was he temporarily insane, allowing his body to make decisions rather than his mind? How did his heart figure into it all?

"You couldn't have been more wrong," he said, "when you accused me of having a string of women. It's just the opposite, in fact. I'm thirty-three years old and I've only been with one woman in my entire life. Since kindergarten, all those years, I never even looked at anybody else but Jenny. It never occurred to me. Not even after she died. I thought I was content. I thought there never could be anybody else. And then…"

He sighed. Maybe it was love if love walked in wearing slinky blue velvet and spiked heels. "And then you walked into my life."

"Lucky me," she said with more than a hint of sarcasm in her tone.

"Yeah," Sam laughed softly. "Lucky you."

He shifted his weight in the seat, but didn't loosen his hold on her. Now that the storm was over, he was so afraid she'd bolt.

"Just come back, Laura. Please," he said. "At least until you've got someplace else to go."

She sighed, a long, wet and weary exhalation which Sam took for acquiescence.

"Good," he said before she had time to change her mind.

He was about to straighten up and start the car when a single headlight beamed just a way down the road. Damn. If he'd told Janey once, he'd told her a dozen times that she needed to get that broken light fixed. It wasn't safe, driving out here in the country, with a single beam. Not for her or Samantha.

Laura began to rise up.

"Stay down just a sec," he said, pressing his hand on her shoulder. "Janey's coming. No sense setting her off."

Oh, by all means, let's not upset poor Janey.

In spite of Sam's admonition, Laura was tempted to pop up behind the steering wheel, right in Sam's lap, like a leering jack-in-the-box, if only to see the look on the woman's face.

Janey's voice was tight, wound up, so full of phony cheer that Laura nearly gagged. She had driven right over to give him the good news, Janey told Sam. Samantha's tests came back from the hospital and there was no indication of meningitis. None whatsoever. Now there was a surprise, Laura thought uncharitably, even as Sam was offering a convincing sigh of relief.

Wouldn't he like to come over for dinner to celebrate? Just the three of them? No, he didn't think that would be possible. Not this week, anyway. There was this case...

The *case* in question almost laughed out loud in the vicinity of his belt buckle. Why did he continue to be so nice to her? Why in the world didn't he just come out and say "Take a hike, Janey"?

The answer to that was simple enough. It was because he was Sam. Because he seemed genetically incapable of saying no when somebody needed him. Because he was true blue and loyal and chock-full of all the good qualities that Laura had thought no longer existed. So, while Janey pressed and pressed, Sam dithered and demurred and declined her invitations until she was finally forced to give up. Well, not quite.

"Samantha misses you so much, Sam," she crooned.

"I miss her, too. Give her a kiss for me, will you? I'll stop by once business calms down. I promise."

"Next week?" Janey asked, not missing a beat or a chance to pin him down.

"Probably."

"Tuesday?"

Give it a rest Laura wanted to scream.

"I'll see. Get that headlight fixed, Janey, okay?"

"Sure. Okay. Maybe Tuesday, then. Samantha will be so happy. I'll call to remind you. See you, Sam."

With Sam's hand still heavy on her shoulder, Laura could hear gravel spit from under Janey's tires when she wheeled her car around and drove back the way she had come. Laura imagined that sole headlight burning with an almost demented light, like a cyclops driven wild by what he couldn't reach.

"The coast is clear," Sam said, sounding as if he'd been hunkered down in a foxhole with bullets whizzing over his head for the past few minutes.

Laura sat up, plucking at the damp sleeves of her T-shirt and the knees of her jeans, battling with her need to tell Sam just how wrong he was to think his kindness was anything but misguided or even dangerous where Janey Sayles was concerned. A woman who would use her own defenseless daughter to get his attention was probably capable of anything, and Laura was more convinced than ever that Janey was behind the curling iron incident and the vandalized tomatoes. If only Sam could see...

"Thanks," he said quietly. "If it makes you feel any better, Laura, I think you're probably right about Janey."

"You do?"

Sam nodded, then muttered an oath. "Yeah. And I bet you think I'm the world's biggest coward, don't you?"

"No." She leaned over to kiss his cheek. "I think you're the world's sweetest coward, Sam Zachary."

While Sam tended the storm-battered rose bushes in the front yard, Laura went inside to change out of her wet clothes. Her indignant huff had lasted all of half an hour. Not an easy man to walk out on, her sweet, cowardly Sam.

She put her toothbrush back in the bathroom, glanced at the damp mop of curls on her head, then at the charred vanity top, and profoundly wished that Janey had chosen something other than the curling iron with which to wreak her havoc earlier. Why hadn't she just sprayed shaving cream all over the place or short-sheeted the beds?

Well, that was simple enough to figure out. Because then Sam wouldn't have blamed Laura for burning down his house. If they had nothing else in common, at least she and Sam shared the privilege of being stalked by firebugs.

But from now on Sam would be wary of the woman, she thought while trotting down the stairs. Who knows? He might even work up the courage to tell her to buzz off, although Laura doubted it. His streak of loyalty, which she found so endearing, seemed to apply to enemies and stalkers as much as it did to old loves and old houses and all the junk inside them.

She stood at the bottom of the stairs a moment, gazing into the living room with all its glass gewgaws and porcelain knickknacks, while the kernel of an idea began to take shape in her head. Sam had enough collectibles and old clothes to stock a small retail outlet, while she was a retailer plumb out of stock. Would he consider being her partner, she wondered?

No. Probably not. He hadn't shown much interest earlier when she'd broached the subject of selling his mother's clothes. On the other hand, he didn't exactly strike Laura as Private Eye of the Year. He showed far more enthusiasm for his silly garden than he did for his occupation.

It couldn't hurt to ask, she decided. She had to do

something, after all. She couldn't continue living on Sam's generosity indefinitely.

In the kitchen, she glanced at the clock. It was a little after five, time for all good cooks to stoke up their ovens, fire their burners, and drag out their chopping boards. Okay. So she wasn't a good cook. So she'd chickened out at breakfast this morning when threatened by seventeen kinds of cheese. That didn't mean she couldn't come up with something halfway edible for dinner.

The plastic bowl brimming with rescued tomatoes caught her eye, and inspiration struck. Anybody could slice tomatoes, right? A little salt. A pinch of pepper. A slosh of salad dressing. How hard was that? She pulled out a drawer in search of a knife just as the phone rang.

When it was obvious, after five or six rings, that Sam wasn't going to come bounding through the door to answer it, Laura picked up the receiver and said hello.

"Yes, ma'am. It's Ms. McNeal, right?"

"Yes," Laura answered. "Who is...?"

"This is Officer Charlie Travis, ma'am. I met you this morning when I was checking out that prowler report."

"Oh, sure. I hope you're calling to say you found him and arrested him."

"Well, no. Not exactly. Is Sam around? I really need to talk to him."

"He's outside someplace," Laura said, peering out the window over the sink and then looking out the back door, but failing to see Sam. "If you want to hang on, I'll go out and give him a shout, Officer."

"How about if you just have him call me back?" the man said. "I'm at home. He's got my number."

"Okay. I'll tell him."

"I appreciate that, ma'am. Tell him to call as soon as possible, will you? It's pretty important."

After she hung up, Laura stepped out the back door. Sam was carrying an armload of greenery across the yard.

"Careful," he called to her. "Watch out for the wolf spiders."

"Very funny," she yelled, glancing nervously at the ground around her feet. "You just got a phone call."

"Be right there. Let me just toss these on the mulch pile."

A mulch pile! Laura sighed as she stepped back inside. This was like living in a foreign country. How in the world could she be falling for somebody who had a mulch pile?

The thought brought her up short halfway to the sink. She wasn't falling for Sam. She was grateful, that was all. He was providing protection and offering her shelter. He was sweet and loyal and extraordinarily nice to look at, but she wasn't falling for him. Okay. So he was fabulous in bed, too, and made her feel things she'd never felt before. That was sex, not love.

She was *not* falling in love with him. She was never going to fall in love with anybody. Not only that, she wasn't going to start doing cutesy things in the kitchen like making rosebuds out of radishes or silly carrot curls. Good grief. All this country air must be rotting her brain.

She stood glaring at the tomatoes on the counter

when the phone rang again. Now what? Laura glared at the phone, too, almost hoping it was Janey calling this time so she could have the pleasure of hanging up on her. She snatched the receiver off the hook and muttered hello just as Sam came in the back door.

"Laura?" the voice on the other end of the line said in response to her surly greeting. "Laura, doll, is that you?"

Artie! Oh, my God.

"It's Artie," she rasped with her hand covering the mouthpiece.

Sam looked at her as if he had suddenly gone deaf and extremely dumb. "Who? Who is it?"

"Artie," she whispered. "Oh, God, Sam. Here."

She tossed the phone at him as if it were a live grenade, then paced back and forth from the door to the window while she listened to Sam murmur a series of calm and noncommittal *uh-huhs* and *okays* and *sure things* before he finally offered a cheerful "Great. See you then," and hung up.

"He knows I'm here," Laura said, coming to a standstill in the middle of the kitchen, attempting to keep her voice out of its highest, hysterical registers.

Sam didn't answer immediately, but stood gnawing on his lower lip, gazing out the window, presumably lost in thought, hopefully coming up with a plan to ensure her survival. She was already mentally grabbing her toothbrush and shopping bags again, preparing to flee.

"Well?" Laura asked, no longer able to disguise her impatience or her rising anxiety. "I can't stand the suspense, Sam. Tell me. What did Artie say? He knew it was me, didn't he?"

Sam's gaze swung from the window to her. "He

recognized your voice. He said I must be one hell of a detective to have found you so fast.''

"Oh, great. That's just great." Laura rolled her eyes. "What else?"

"And he said I had earned a handsome bonus for my excellent work." He waggled his eyebrows, much to Laura's irritation.

"Wonderful," she snapped. "I couldn't be more pleased for you. And just when does he intend to give you this handsome bonus?"

"Tomorrow," he said. "He's expecting us in his office at noon."

She was certain she hadn't heard him right. Either that, or it had been a slip of the tongue. "You mean Artie's expecting *you*, don't you?"

"No. I mean us. You and me. At noon."

Chapter 11

While he was telling her about the meeting with Artie, Sam could actually see the color drain from Laura's face. She wobbled, looking ill, but when he reached out to steady her, she slapped his hands away.

"Traitor," she barked. "I should have known that's why you didn't want me to leave. How much is he paying you?"

He took a step back, raising his hands helplessly. "Wait a minute. Whoa. You don't really think I'd..."

But apparently she did. Her eyes glittered like blue ice when she cut him off with, "No. I thought I was safe. I thought you were different from everybody else, Sam. I thought you were better. The best. Boy, was I wrong!"

"Laura," he protested, "I'm not..."

"How much is good old Artie paying you to turn me over to him, you Judas?" she screeched.

"Judas!" He ripped his fingers through his hair. "I'm jeopardizing my investigator's license, my only source of income, and you're calling me a Judas? I don't believe this."

He yanked a chair out from the table. "Will you just sit and listen to me for two minutes?"

Laura eyed the chair as if it might be booby-trapped.

"Please," Sam said. He gave the chair a little shake. "Just sit."

"This better be good," she said, brushing past him to perch on the very edge of the seat, tense as a sprinter just before the starting gun.

Sam lowered himself into the chair across from her. "I am not turning you over to Artie."

"But you said—"

He raised a hand to silence her. "I said we're meeting with him. Frankly, I don't see that we have any other choice now that he knows where you are."

"I'll leave." She sat back and crossed her arms.

"Yeah. That's one option, I guess. But then I'd have to leave, too, and I really don't want to do that."

Some of the flintiness went out of her eyes. "You'd do that?"

He wanted to shake her almost as much as he wanted to wrap his arms around her. "Of course, I'd do that. What did I just say to you in the car only a half hour ago? Were you even listening?"

"You asked me not to go. At least until I had somewhere *to* go."

"I said a hell of a lot more than that," he muttered

irritably. Why didn't women ever listen, he wondered? Why didn't they understand him? He spoke English, didn't he? Why didn't Janey get it? Or Laura?

"I care about you, dammit," he said.

Why Laura tilted back her head and laughed at that, Sam had no idea. It wasn't funny to him.

"Oh, Sam," she said on a long sigh. "I care about you, too. That's probably why I don't want you to totally disrupt your life for me or jeopardize your investigator's license when you won't even remember my name a year or two from now."

"What? I just don't get it, Laura. Do you think I have some sort of mental deficiency? Some problem with my long-term memory?"

She shook her head. "No, I don't think you have any deficiencies at all. It's me. I'm the one with the long-term problem. Men...well, they walk out on me."

Her shoulders rose and fell in a shrug. "I don't know. I should probably just solve this whole horrible thing with Artie by saying yes to him and then waiting for the rotten creep to take the inevitable powder."

The idea alone was enough to tighten the muscles in Sam's shoulders and neck, and to turn his stomach sour. He was already worried enough about the possibility of violence in tomorrow's encounter. Not Artie's violence so much as his own. He rolled his neck to loosen a few of the knots, then said, "I've never walked out on a woman in my life."

"That's because there *was* only one woman," she shot back.

"I rest my case." Sam grinned.

Laura cocked her head to one side, staring at him a long while before she said, "What exactly did you have in mind with this meeting tomorrow?"

"Well, see, a guy like our friend Artie isn't deterred by threats of physical violence. In fact, the more he's threatened, I suspect, the bigger and meaner and better he feels. So I was thinking we'd appeal to his innate sense of morality."

"You're assuming he has one," she said.

"Okay. Then, call it his territorial instinct."

"What does that mean?"

"In a nutshell, it means that when I tell him you're my woman, he'll have the good sense to stay away from you."

"And if that doesn't work?" she asked.

Sam shrugged. "Then, I'll just deck him and be done with it. Either way, he won't be bothering you anymore."

Sam's woman.

Even though it was a fiction, it had a certain appeal, Laura decided while she sat watching him as he prepared to turn the salvaged tomatoes into spaghetti sauce. There was something about a hunk in a blue gingham apron, two hundred pounds of dense bone and solid muscle decked with ruffles and bows, that kept sending little ripples through her bloodstream and making her heart nearly itch with desire.

My God, she was even paying attention as he gathered the ingredients for the spaghetti sauce. No. Sorry. The *Bolognese* sauce. Well, almost *Bolognese*. When Sam confessed that he didn't have any chicken livers on hand, fresh or frozen, he had such a look of disappointment on his face that Laura altered her jubilant "Thank God!" to a wistful "Aw, gee."

She sidled up to stand beside him at the sink where he was running tomatoes under a spray of water from the faucet. Ordinarily, the kitchen sink was not her favorite place to be, but with Sam close at her side, it was suddenly akin to standing before that famous fountain in Rome, the one where visitors tossed coins and made wishes. Oh, how she wished...

"Can I help?" she asked, afraid to wish for what she couldn't have. Or, more precisely, what she couldn't keep.

"Sure. Here." He plopped one big fat tomato in her hand and then another. "How about blanching these?"

"You got it."

She pondered the red, succulent globes a moment. Blanching? Blanching? All she knew to do to tomatoes was slice the suckers, so she decided that blanching was obviously just a fancy word for that.

"Where's the knife?" she asked.

"What for?"

"To slice...I mean, to blanch them with."

Sam grabbed back his tomatoes, the expression on his face wavering somewhere between horror and hilarity.

"How about just opening up a bottle of wine?" he suggested.

Laura looked heavenward. "You must think I'm such a boob." She started to turn, to go back to her seat at the table where she obviously belonged, but Sam caught her in his arms.

"I think you're the best thing that's happened to me in a long, long time," he said, nudging her chin up, coaxing her gaze to meet his. "So, you're not exactly comfortable in a kitchen. What difference does that make?"

Absolutely none at the moment, she thought, when she was oh so comfortable in his arms, so cozy in the warm light of his eyes. Sam widened his stance, leaning back against the counter, drawing her closer against him, dispelling any notion that she might have had that beneath the ruffled gingham apron there was anything but hard masculine heat.

He bent his head, brushing his lips softly against hers, sampling one corner of her mouth with his tongue, driving her utterly wild.

"How hungry are you?" he whispered huskily.

"Famished," she answered in a voice nearly as sultry as his, rising on tiptoe as she spoke to be nearer, closer. "Ravenous."

"Me, too." He deepened the kiss deliriously, then quit just long enough to murmur, "We weren't going to... You asked me not to do this, remember?"

No. She barely remembered her own name. "I must've been out of my mind," she groaned.

"Are you now?"

As he spoke, Sam was tugging her T-shirt from her jeans. His big hands cradled her rib cage a moment and his tongue tantalized her ear. "Are you out of your mind now?"

"Completely," she managed to say while she reciprocated by wrenching up the back of his shirt so she could feel the smooth, bewitching warmth of his skin. Oh, how she adored the slight give to it before her fingertips met solid muscle. How she loved the shiver even her lightest touch seemed to provoke.

"Me, too," Sam said just before a wolfish growl

rumbled deep in his throat and he swept her up into his arms. "We need a bed," he muttered against her ear. "I'm getting too old for that floor stuff."

The phone on the far wall jangled, earning a sigh from Laura and a gruff curse from Sam. It suddenly occurred to her that after the shock of Artie's call, she had forgotten to give Sam the message from Officer Charlie.

"Let it ring," he said.

"Wait, Sam. I was supposed to tell you to call Charlie. He said he was at home. I'm sorry. It sounded important."

"It damn well better be," he muttered, glaring in the direction of the phone and lowering Laura to the floor before he stalked to answer it. Then, after barely thirty seconds of conversation, he pointed to the light switch on the far wall and ordered Laura to hit it.

"Why?" she asked.

"Just do it," he snapped. "Now."

She was reaching up to the switch just as the window over the sink seemed to explode and glass flew everywhere.

"Get over here," Sam yelled into the phone almost at the same time that he yelled for Laura to get down.

Not needing to be told once, let alone twice, she was already halfway to the floor, intending to make herself one with the linoleum. Sam hit the light switch, then crouched beside her in the dark. She wasn't sure if it was his heart thundering or her own. Probably both.

"It's Artie," she whispered. "Isn't it?"

"No. It's Janey."

* * *

The squad car screeched into the driveway a fast five minutes later, but in the meantime Sam had moved a terrified Laura to the relative safety of the interior hallway, even though he was already convinced that the shot, like the curling iron and the vandalized tomatoes before it, was just an isolated warning. He really didn't expect Janey to try to come into the house and finish what she had started.

"Sam!" Charlie's voice sounded just outside the shattered window. "You okay in there?"

"Yeah. We're fine."

"Well, if she was here," Charlie called, "she's long gone now. Probably parked over at the Beeman place and cut across their field."

Beside him, Laura whispered in a tiny, frantic voice, "She's gone? Is that what he said? It's okay to get up now? Are you sure?"

"Stay here a minute, just in case," Sam said.

He flipped on the light in the kitchen and surveyed the glass-littered sink and countertop and floor, hardly concerned about the mess when he considered the alternative. Only moments before Janey had fired, he and Laura had been perfect targets, standing at the window, kissing, tearing at each other's clothes, oblivious to everything but the heat roaring between them. He should have had more sense than that.

"Oh, my God." Laura stood nearby, her fingertips lightly touching his arm. "Oh, Sam."

From her tone, it was obvious that she had reached the same conclusion. They were lucky to be alive. Then Charlie came in the back door, and the three of them stood there, pondering the wreckage.

"Hell, I knew something was up when I heard that Janey was making a damned nuisance of herself at one gun shop after another this afternoon," Charlie said. "I guess I should've come straight over here when you didn't call me back right away. I'm real sorry about that, Sam."

"Not your fault. You couldn't have anticipated this." Sam waved a hand across the glass strewn floor. "Nobody could," he said, contrary to what he was telling himself, that *he* should have anticipated it, that *he* should have realized that Janey was capable of anything. Even this.

"You're going to arrest her, right?" Laura asked, picking a shard of glass out of the sink and dropping it into the trash.

"Well..." Charlie murmured. "That all depends on what sort of evidence we can come up with. And mostly it depends on Sam, here."

"On Sam? What do you mean?" She looked to Sam for a reply.

"He means if I decide to press charges, Laura."

"You have to," she insisted. "You can't let that woman get away with this."

"It's pretty hard proving what actually happened here, ma'am," Charlie offered. "There's what we all know, but that doesn't count for squat without the physical evidence." He stretched out a foot to take a swat at a piece of glass. "The sheriff, Sam's replacement, isn't one to waste manpower on hunting and gathering if it doesn't get him a spot on the front page of the paper or his face on the six o'clock news."

"The woman is crazy," Laura said. "Good Lord. There's no telling what she might do next."

Charlie shrugged helplessly.

"Well, we're not going to wait around to find

out," Sam said. "Get your stuff together, Laura. Charlie, do me a favor, will you, and call the board-up people and have them send somebody over here as soon as possible to take care of that window?"

"Sure thing, boss," the officer replied. "If they can't get to it tonight, I'll see to it myself."

"Thanks. And one other thing. See if you can locate Wes Gunther and give him a heads-up on this. Tell him he might want to think about trying to get custody of his daughter, at least for the time being."

"Right," Charlie said. "You got any idea yet where you'll be?"

Sam shook his head. "No, none, but I'll let you know when we get there."

There turned out to be an antiquated motel, or more precisely a little clutch of pine-log tourist cabins, called Havenrest. The middle "n," Laura noticed, had burned out on the blue neon sign, but "Have rest" wasn't such a bad name for a place where they could safely hide out from rotten Artie and crazy Janey.

She followed Sam into the larger log cabin designated "Office" where an elderly gentleman sat watching a silent baseball game on an ancient console television that was nearly as big as the cabins out back. When he saw them come through the door, the man hauled himself out his rocking chair and called out hoarsely, "Hortense, we've got company."

"Evening," Sam said.

The old geezer cupped a hand to his ear. "What's that?"

"I said good evening," Sam repeated, louder this time, but to no avail. The man stared at him blankly.

A little gnome of a woman with a cloud of snow white hair emerged from a door behind the registration desk. She reminded Laura of Mrs. Santa Claus until she boomed out, "It don't do no good yelling, young man. His battery's dead."

"What's that?" the old man said.

The little woman shot him a fierce and no doubt well-practiced glare that immediately sent him shuffling back to his rocker and the muted baseball game.

"We'd like a room," Sam said.

"You would, would you?" She trained an equally fierce glare on Sam, arced it toward Laura briefly, then back to Sam. "Are you kids married?"

"No," he said.

"Yes," Laura piped up at the same instant.

"Well, which is it?" she demanded while she gripped her registration book like a holy relic. "I don't mind waiting while the two of you get your stories straight."

It seemed fairly obvious to Laura that the woman wasn't going to let them set foot in one of her precious cabins if they weren't man and wife, so she gave Sam a little nudge with her elbow and was about to cross her fingers behind her back and lie like a rug when he announced, "We're not married, ma'am. If that's a problem for you, we'll just go someplace else."

Laura was ready to turn and walk out the door they had just come in when the woman let out a whoop and said, "Good for you! I like an honest man. And if you're smart, you'll stay that way, too. Single, I mean. You, too, Missy. The both of you."

"What's that, Hortense?" the man in the rocker shouted across the little lobby while he tapped at the contraption in his ear.

"Your battery's dead, Herman," she yelled, then muttered under her breath, "Been dead since I married you, you durn fool." She gave a snort and turned the registration book around, then handed Sam a pen. "Sign right here, young man."

The woman didn't bat an eye when Sam signed the page with a sweeping "Mr. and Mrs. Alexander Hamilton" or when he counted out the forty-eight dollars for the cost of their accommodations.

"Cabin Six," she said, pushing a key across the countertop. "Don't worry about making noise. Herman over there won't hear and I won't mind one bit."

"We'll be quiet," Sam said, grasping Laura's arm and leading her toward the door. "G'night."

"And you remember what I said about staying single," the woman called.

As the door closed on the office, Laura could hear poor old Herman inquire once more, "What's that?"

Laughing, she slipped her arm through Sam's as they crossed the parking lot, suddenly feeling lighter and brighter, not quite so hunted anymore. "I don't think Hortense is too keen on holy matrimony," she said.

Sam grinned and cupped a hand to his ear. "What's that?"

She laughed harder, clutching his arm tighter. For somebody in a world of trouble, Laura marveled that she could do anything but cry. And now, because of her, poor Sam was in a world of trouble, too.

Cabin Six turned out to be set off from numbers

One through Five by a dilapidated playground where the sandbox was full of leaves and paper trash, where gangly weeds had sprouted up beneath the swing seats that hung from rusty chains. It had probably been years since any child had played here, since little feet had worn the ground to dust along the bottom arc of a swing.

She had a sudden vision of her father, standing behind her, pushing her shoulders, sending her higher and higher toward the sky while he laughed and told her to point her toes and kick the devil out of the clouds. His face appeared so vivid, so real in every detail that it surprised Laura since the image of her father had been excised from all family photographs for decades, the way his name had been banished from all conversation.

For one bleak, nearly unbearable moment she missed him terribly.

Sam stopped all of a sudden. "What's wrong?" he asked, turning her to him and searching her face.

All she could do just then was shake her head. Even so, it didn't dislodge the poignant vision of the young, smiling Oliver McNeal. Daddy.

"Don't be afraid," he said, tightening his grip on her shoulders. "This is the last place on earth anybody would look for us, Laura. And even if they did, I wouldn't let anybody hurt you."

"It's not that." She could barely speak for the sudden lump in her throat. "It's… I was looking at the playground and thinking about my father. I haven't thought about him much. Not really. Not in years. And now suddenly…"

Hot tears welled up in her eyes. Laura swiped them away. "This is so stupid. I'll be fine."

"Is he dead?" Sam asked.

"What?"

"Your father. The first man to walk out on you." He thumbed a tear from her cheek. "Is he dead or alive?"

"I don't know. My mother never talked about him after he left. She got angry if I asked."

"Do you want to know?"

Laura blinked. "I never thought..."

"Well, think about it," Sam said. "That's what I do, you know. Find people."

Suddenly the mere idea that it might be possible to find him, to somehow reattach her dad to all those mutilated family photographs, seemed to lift a burden from her heart.

She could feel a smile actually take possession of her lips.

"Oh, Sam! You really could find him, couldn't you?"

He nodded.

"I don't have all that much information about him. What would you need? Name, date of birth, Social Security number? Maybe I could..."

"Slow down." He pulled her arm through his and continued toward Cabin Six. "We'll get started on it tomorrow, okay? In the meantime... Home sweet home."

Sam turned the key in the lock and pushed in the knotty pine door. He stuck his head in, looked around, then stepped back to announce almost gleefully, "What a dump. You're really going to love this, honey."

Thank God for gold shag carpets, lava lamps, and bedspreads decked with pink flamingoes, Sam thought. He had sensed a sadness coming over Laura as they crossed the parking lot, and he simply couldn't bear the idea of her being sad. It made his heart feel like a rock in his chest.

For the first time since he'd gotten his crummy P.I. license, he took some real pleasure in the occupation. He'd find her father for her, hopefully not in some cemetery, but alive and eager to make up for all the damage he'd done to his little girl. In the meantime, however, there was this godawful room to delight her. If it hadn't, Sam decided, he would've stood on his head in a knotty pine paneled corner and whistled "Dixie" just to make her smile.

And smile she did, just like a kid in a candy store.

"Oh, Sam. Look at this." She held up a queasy green plastic ashtray, molded in the shape of a boomerang. "Isn't it great?"

"Great," he echoed as enthusiastically as he could.

"And look at this TV," she exclaimed. "Rabbit ears! Do you believe it?"

"I wouldn't turn it on, if I were you," he said. "I'll bet it only picks up *The Twilight Zone*."

She shivered, more out of delight than fright, then continued to happily explore their pine-paneled environment while Sam took a seat on the edge of one of the twin beds and reached for the big, black rotary phone on the nightstand.

"I'm going to call Charlie and let him know where we are," he said.

It occurred to him, though, that he also wanted to ask some questions regarding Janey's whereabouts that he really didn't want Laura to overhear for fear they would spoil her current mood, so he delved in his pocket to see how much change he could come up with. Five quarters weren't going to get them a feast from the vending machines, even at '50s prices.

He waved a five-dollar bill in Laura's direction. "Think you've got the strength to ask Herman for some change?"

She tugged at her earlobe. "What's that?" Then she laughed as she took the money from his hand.

"Very funny. I'm starving. Why don't you see what you can come up with in the way of dinner from those vending machines in the office."

"You got it." She laughed again as she headed for the door. "I'm a vending machine kind of girl, in case you haven't noticed."

Sam smiled. "I noticed."

He noticed, too, that when Laura left, she took all her weird, sweet magic with her and the room reverted to what it truly was. A dump. He couldn't help but think that's how his whole life would look without this woman in it.

Laura stood with a handful of quarters in front of the vending machines, trying to decide whether Sam, with his gourmet tendencies, would prefer barbecued potato chips or plain, ruffled or flat, when she happened to glance at the screen of Herman's television just as the baseball game blinked off and was replaced by a headline reading Special Report.

Suddenly, on the screen, was someone who bore an amazing resemblance to Sam's friend, Officer Travis. A local reporter was holding a microphone in front of his worried face.

"Turn it up," Laura said.

"What's that?"

"Turn it... Never mind." She pocketed her quarters, hurried around the old man's rocker, and turned up the sound herself.

...and in your opinion, then, the woman is indeed armed and capable of carrying out her threat? Is that correct, Officer?

That's correct. We have reason to believe that she is in possession of at least one firearm.

And the child the Sayles woman is holding hostage? Can you give us any information about that?

The hostage is a female, approximately three years of age. Samantha.

Her own daughter, is that correct?

Yes.

Exactly what is the woman demanding?

I'm not at liberty to say at the present time.

We've heard rumors that it has something to do with Sam Zachary, the former county sheriff. Can you confirm that?

No comment.

"Oh, my God," Laura gasped as the reporter turned a somber face to the camera.

And so the nightmare of little Samantha continues. We'll break in with further developments. Back to you in the studio, Paul.

Chapter 12

Sam got pulled over for speeding, which was exactly what he'd intended when he jammed his foot hard on the Blazer's accelerator and sent cinders flying as he peeled out of the motel parking lot. The Havenrest was hell and gone on the opposite side of the county from Janey's house, which was the exact reason he had chosen it. But now that he needed to get back there, it would have taken an extra fifteen minutes without a police escort.

"This isn't your fault, Sam," Laura said as if she were reading his mind. "You couldn't have known she'd do something so completely off-the-wall."

He kept his eyes on the road and the flashing lights mounted on the cruiser just ahead. "It is my fault. I should have suspected something like this with Janey getting more unstable every day. If anything happens to that little girl…"

"It won't. I'm sure of that. It's just Janey's sick way of getting your attention."

"Well, she's got it."

Sam scowled through the windshield, not knowing what to expect once he arrived on the scene, feeling helpless in the face of Janey's demands, whatever they turned out to be. He only knew one thing. Nobody was going to get hurt during this debacle. Not Samantha and not Janey, either. He'd do whatever he had to in order to prevent that.

He tried to imagine all the possible scenarios that awaited him, running them through his head, deciding how he might deal with each one, all the while knowing it was an exercise in futility when it was Janey who ultimately would decide the outcome of tonight's events.

Predictably, the scene was utter chaos when they arrived with countless sheriff's department vehicles, two EMS units, and three local television trucks, beaming the entire Chinese fire drill back to their stations. God only knows how many civilian gawkers there were, sitting on hoods of cars and camped out in lawn chairs. Even that lousy ambulance chaser and quick-buck artist, Louie, had arrived with his snack truck, ready to serve the curious masses coffee and doughnuts at inflated prices.

"What a zoo," Laura said.

"Yep. Just the way Ed Harrelson likes it," Sam snarled, pulling on the emergency brake. "The current sheriff has a tendency to confuse publicity with good law enforcement."

"What do you want me to do, Sam?" Laura asked, lifting a hand to shield her eyes from all the flashing lights.

"I want you to stay right here," he said. "I'll leave the keys in the ignition. If anything happens…"

Her eyes widened perceptibly and locked on his. "Don't even say that."

"Hey." He took her sweet, fearful face in both his hands. "Nothing's going to happen. I promise. But you remember Charlie, right?"

She nodded.

"Well, just tell him your situation. He's a good guy. He'll know what to do."

"You're a good guy," she whispered. "I wish you didn't…"

"Shh. Me, too, babe." He leaned forward and kissed her softly, wishing he never had to stop, hoping like hell he wasn't kissing her goodbye.

After she lost sight of Sam's broad shoulders in the crowd, Laura moved over to the driver's seat just to feel his warmth lingering in the leather upholstery.

He'll be fine, she kept telling herself. Janey wasn't going to shoot him. She loved him, for heaven's sake. But the thought that should have been such a comfort turned frightening when she remembered Artie's angry proclamation. *If I can't have you, then by God nobody else will either.*

She reached to turn the key so she could lower her window, then craned her neck to catch one more glimpse of Sam.

"Looking for Sam?"

At the sound of the female voice, Laura jerked her head around and came face-to-face with a woman she recognized instantly, but no matter how hard she wracked her brain, she couldn't attach a name to the pretty face framed by soft brown hair, the perfect teeth, the delicate indentation in the chin. Was she a customer from Nana's Attic? No, not in that silk designer suit. Somebody who owned an antique store on Russell Boulevard? Who?

"I'm sorry." Laura felt like an idiot. "I know you, I'm sure I do, but I can't..."

The woman's quick laughter cut her off. "That's okay. I'm Linda Sturgis, Channel Five News. Don't feel bad. Everybody knows the face, but the name usually doesn't kick in for a few minutes."

"Oh, sure. I'm sorry it didn't click at first." Laura immediately envisioned the Sturgis woman behind the huge polished sweep of a television newsroom desk, sitting beside her male counterpart, What's-his-name, the one whose face looked as if it had been sculpted out of Ivory soap.

"I saw you drive up with Sam," the woman said as she ran her perfectly shaped and painted fingertips along the edge of the window glass. "Let me guess. You're the reason dear old Janey finally went off the rails."

Laura blinked. "Well, I don't know if that's true or not."

Dear old Janey? That didn't strike Laura as an observation from a professional journalist, exactly. It sounded personal. Almost too personal. Those long fingernails tracing the window frame began to look more like claws.

"Don't worry," Linda Sturgis said with a wave of one of those finely manicured hands. "This isn't going on the ten o'clock news. Trust me. I'm just curious. I had a thing for Sam when he was sheriff here." She laughed. "Me and half the reporters in town. Whenever anything newsworthy happened out here, my God, we'd nearly trample one another at the station to get the assignment.''

"Oh.''

It seemed a safe enough response. Far more genteel, Laura thought, than hitting the window switch and crushing the woman's claws between the glass and the door frame. Right now the woman was studying Laura's face as if it were under a microscope. "Well, I guess you've known Sam for a long time, then?'' she asked, not knowing what else to say.

"Never as well as I wanted to. Well, he was seriously involved with that prima donna pianist.'' Linda Sturgis shrugged. "Funny. I always assumed Crazy Janey was hanging around Sam as her sister's attack dog, sent to keep other interested females at bay.'' She angled her head toward the house in the direction Sam had gone. "This little incident puts it all in a brand new light, I guess. Crazy Janey appears to have a mind of her own, psychotic as it is, not to mention a definite agenda of her own. Mind if I ask your name?''

Laura minded very much. The last thing she needed in her current situation was publicity. "I'd rather not say,'' she replied.

"That's fine. It's off-the-record, honest. I'm just curious. How long have you known Sam?''

"About a week.''

"Ooh. You do quick work,'' the reporter said with an appreciative little leer. "So, then, I assume you didn't know the other sister. *La Grande* Jenny.''

Laura shook her head.

"That's too bad. I thought maybe you could clarify something I was really curious about.'' She grinned, leaning closer to the window, lowering her voice. "I was always dying to know if she took her tiara off when she went to bed with him."

Not only did the remark strike Laura as offensive, but the idea of anybody else in Sam's bed had her hands almost curling in fists. She turned away from the reporter to peer in the direction of the house, hoping for even a small glimpse of him. Where was he? What was happening?

"Don't worry," Linda Sturgis said. "Even if he does go in, it'll take a while to get everything in place."

"If he goes in?" Laura echoed.

"Sure. That's what Crazy Janey's demanding. The kid comes out if Sam goes in. You didn't know that?"

"No. I didn't." The words came out as little more than breath.

"So, anyway, are you and Sam…?"

"Excuse me." Laura opened the truck's door so fast that it nearly knocked the reporter off her feet.

"Yeah. Well. I guess that pretty much answers my question," the woman called as Laura hurried away.

"I'm calling the shots here, Sam, and you're not going in there until I say you're going in. Do you hear me?"

Ed Harrelson stopped just short of poking his finger into the Kevlar vest that Sam was strapping on, and Sam was trying hard not to swat the wiry little rodent out of his way. No wonder just about every guy in the department had begged Sam to run for the job again. Ed wasn't a sheriff. He was a goddamned master of ceremonies.

"You need to get your men in place, Ed," Sam said quietly, dredging up what little patience he could. "I'll hand the little girl out the window on the south side of the house. There. The one with the missing shutter. Somebody's got to be there to take her the minute I open the window."

Sam had just gotten off the phone with Janey whose grip on reality sounded tenuous at best. Jenny, she claimed, was ordering her to do this. Jenny was furious about the bimbo, the slut, the sleazy blonde that Sam had allowed into his house. Jenny was going to make Janey hurt Samantha in order for Sam to see the error of his ways. She wanted to see Sam. Alone. Now.

"I'm not so sure about that particular window," Ed said. "See, the lights are all set up out here in front. We've got at least a quarter of a million people... What time is it?" He shot his gold watch from the sleeve of his dress uniform. "Hell, by ten o'clock we could have half a million people sitting on the edge of their seats, holding their breath, wanting to see that the kid's all right."

"Which window are we talking about, Sheriff Harrelson?" asked a guy with a mini cam balanced on his shoulder. "If it's not in front, then we're going to need a little extra time to move some of our lights."

"See," Harrelson muttered to Sam.

He wanted to jerk the little publicity hound up by his pressed lapels and tell him he was working for the county, dammit, not Channels Five, Six and Eight, and that if he didn't do this right, the film at eleven was going to be a bloodbath instead of the smooth and efficient rescue of one little girl and the gentle taking into custody of one very sick woman.

Somebody stuck a microphone in Sam's face, and he batted it away. Then somebody put a hand on his arm, and he turned, a curse on his lips, only to see Laura's huge blue eyes in her pale, worried face.

"Hey," he said softly, turning so he stood between her and the house, just in case Janey took another potshot.

"Somebody told me you're going into the house," she said, her gaze taking in the flak jacket then returning to his face. "Do you have to, Sam? Isn't there some other way? Or somebody else?"

"It'll be okay. I've known Janey all her life. I can talk to her."

"And what if she won't listen to you? Then what? My God, she's got a gun."

"That's what this is for." He gestured to the vest.

Laura shivered, rubbing her upper arms, and Sam was just about to reach out to do the same when it suddenly occurred to him that Janey, only a hundred or so yards away in her dark and battened down house, was watching all the commotion in her front yard, seeing everything on television. She'd told him that on the phone. My God. If she saw him standing next to Laura…

Just then a microphone poked between them and a bank of bright lights flared. A woman's voice urgently announced, "This is Linda Sturgis, live at the scene where the hostage drama continues to unfold. I'm speaking with former county sheriff, Sam Zachary. Sam, what's happening?"

Sam swore roughly, unmindful of the tens of thousands of viewers, but thinking of a single desperate and dangerous one, her wild eyes locked on an image of Laura mere inches away from him.

Then a gun went off inside the house. Sam knew instantly that Janey had just blown her rival off the screen.

He had to go in now.

It had been two hours since Sam had thrust Laura at Officer Travis and told him to get her out of sight. Not too long after that, little Samantha had been safely passed through a window, greeted with cheers and applause, then carried to a patrol car and summarily whisked away. To Laura, those two hours felt more like two years.

"It's so damned quiet," she said to Charlie whose head was tipped back against the driver's seat of Sam's Blazer.

He opened his eyes and stared at the house a moment. "That's probably a good sign," he said. "Sam knows what he's doing. A couple of years ago he talked a kid out of jumping from a sixth-floor window."

That didn't really surprise Laura. She thought even if the kid had succeeded in jumping, Sam would have swooped down, cape flying, and carried him safely to the ground. He must have been a wonderfully competent sheriff.

"Why did he quit, Charlie?" she asked, searching for a better answer than Sam's terse *I stopped being good at it.*

The officer did a bit of shifting and squirming, obviously not comfortable with the subject, before he said, "I can't say for certain, mind you, but if I had to come up with a reason, I'd say Sam probably blamed himself for Jenny's death. Janey's sister. His fiancée. You know.''

"I know." An image of a tiara passed through her brain. Laura was quick to dismiss it. "But I thought Jenny was killed in a car accident. Alone. Sam wasn't driving, was he?"

"No. But he heard the call on his radio and was first on the scene. He couldn't get her out. Man, that car was a mess. It took two hours and the Jaws of Life to finally open it up enough to get her body out.''

"Poor Sam."

"Yeah. He was in pretty bad shape. He quit about two weeks after that, I think. Just couldn't hack it. We were all pretty worried about what he might do.''

Laura was wishing she had known Sam then, even though she knew he wouldn't have given her a second glance. "He's better now, don't you think, Charlie? I mean, he seems to have a handle on his grief."

He nodded. "Seems fine to me. That's why I keep pestering him to come back to work. There's an election in two months, and everybody knows Sam would win over Harrelson hands down. It'd be a landslide. Hell, that's probably why Harrelson didn't throw a fit trying to keep him from going in there tonight. He's probably hoping Sam won't walk out."

Laura made a whimpering little sound, and the officer immediately apologized. "Sorry. I didn't mean to upset you, ma'am. He'll come out of there just fine. Probably any minute now. You just watch."

She watched like the proverbial hawk, one with its heart in its throat, all the while thinking about how quickly Sam had become a part of her life. An irreplaceable part. Of all the things she had lost this past week, nothing came even close to the possible loss of Sam. She wondered how that had happened when she'd sworn it never would. She wondered what she ought to do about it. Stay or run like hell?

The scene around Janey's small frame house had taken on the appearance of a siege. Somebody had even had the good sense to bring in a portable potty, Laura noticed, and a snack truck was doing a brisk business with cops and reporters and curious bystanders alike. It seemed more like an impromtu celebration than a potential deathwatch. Suddenly, in spite of all her anxieties, she didn't think she could keep her eyes open another five minutes without the benefit of coffee.

"How about some coffee, Charlie?" Laura tapped her pocket, still stuffed with the vending machine quarters she hadn't had a chance to use back at the Havenrest. "I'm buying."

"Sounds good, but maybe you shouldn't..."

"It's just over there. How do you take it? Cream? Sugar?"

"Black's fine. Thanks."

"Okay. Be back in a jiff."

In the dimness of Janey's bedroom, lit only by the screen of a small black and white TV, Sam surreptitiously checked his watch. It had been two hours since he'd handed a sleepy, but terrified Samantha through the window, and almost an hour since he'd convinced Janey to take a tranquilizer. Her speech patterns and erratic movements had somewhat reverted to normal, and as best as he could determine, her eyelids seemed to be getting a bit heavy.

She'd calmed down considerably since he'd first

come in the house. She was no longer claiming she heard Jenny's voice or that Jenny was making her do these things. But subdued or not, Janey was far from done.

And she still had a fistful of Browning semi-automatic with a probable sixteen or seventeen shots left. One, he figured, had shattered his kitchen window. Another had blown out the screen of the TV in her living room. When this was over, Sam was going to find out what idiot sold the gun to her in her obvious agitated condition and see that the guy wound up selling fireworks in a stall out on Highway 9.

"Jenny didn't love you, Sam," she said for the fiftieth time.

"That's what you said, Janey."

"And you still don't believe me," she shrieked.

"It doesn't make any difference whether I believe you or not. Jenny's dead."

"Thank God for miracles, large and small and all those in between," she muttered with a roll of her eyes and an agitated wave of the pistol. "She didn't deserve you. I don't know why you never understood that. Why you still don't understand. Everybody knew. Everybody."

She turned her gaze to the little television screen where a camera was panning her front yard. "Those ghouls out there. Look at them. Why don't they leave? You're here now. That's all I wanted. That's all I ever wanted."

"They just want to make sure nobody gets hurt," he said, narrowing his eyes on Harrelson, who was deep in conversation with a couple of the SWAT guys. Instinctively, Sam looked to make sure Janey's curtains were drawn tightly closed, thus preventing any dramatic attempts at a head shot to end the stand-off that the publicity-prone sheriff no doubt considered anti-climactic now that Samantha was safely out of the picture.

The camera panned away from Harrelson, across the lawn, then zoomed in on lousy Louie's snack wagon where business was booming. Sam could barely suppress an oath. When he'd been sheriff, he'd ordered Louie to keep a minimum of five hundred yards from any situation in progress, and the first time Louie had disregarded that, Sam had personally flattened all the tires on his movable roach coach and then ticketed him for parking too long in a one-hour zone.

By God, maybe he *would* run for sheriff again this autumn. If Laura objected to living so far out in the country, then he'd get a place in Colterville or Monroe, both well within the county limits. That thought, unbidden, out of the blue, startled him so much that Sam inhaled sharply.

Janey aimed the pistol in his direction. "Don't do anything stupid, Sam. I mean it. I haven't decided yet just what I'm going to do about us."

Neither had Sam, but the threat brought him a bit closer to a decision. It was time to wrap this up, and it had been his intention from the beginning to allow Janey to preserve as much dignity as possible, for her own sake as well as Samantha's. He had hoped that she'd simply get tired and hand over the weapon, then he'd spirit her out the back door and drive her to the hospital.

That wasn't going to happen now.

Crazy Janey was still cruising the outer limits of reality, and he didn't have the expertise to reel her safely in. Unfortunately, he was trained as a soldier, not as a shrink. He could have taken Janey by force the moment he'd walked in with only minimal danger to himself, but he hadn't done it then and he wasn't going to do it now. He wouldn't put her in cuffs and wrestle her outside for half the state to see on their TV screens or for one of Harrelson's snipers to squeeze off a nervous shot at.

His only hope was to render Janey unconscious. And the only way he was going to get close enough to apply the proper choke hold was to kiss her, to draw her willingly into a semilethal embrace.

"What'll it be, miss?"

The man with the grizzled gray hair and greasy T-shirt leaned out of the window at the rear of his truck and pointed his finger at Laura as if it were a gun. He seemed to be having much too good a time, she thought, considering the circumstances.

"Two large coffees," she said. "Both black."

"That'll be three bucks," he told her.

The pirate probably charged extra for cream and sugar. She dug in her pocket for quarters, suddenly picturing Sam sifting teaspoon after teaspoon into his cup. She'd have to wean him away from that nasty habit one of these days and wondered if she'd ever get the chance.

"How long do these hostage deals usually last?" she asked, handing her change up to the man, assuming he was probably an authority on the subject since he ran an affiliated enterprise.

"Depends," he said, leaning forward, shoving aside plastic bottles of mustard and ketchup in order to brace his massive and hairy forearms on the window's little drop-down counter. "I've seen a couple of them take, oh, maybe thirty-six hours or so. Some of them have gone well into a second day."

Laura gave a soft, low whistle. "That's a long time."

"Yep. Most of those long ones, though, were back a couple years ago when we had a different sheriff calling the shots. Now, this Harrelson, the new guy, he's all business. Doesn't coddle crooks the way Sheriff Zachary used to do. Harrelson's more of a shoot first, ask questions later kind of guy."

A voice sounded behind Laura's back. "I'll second that, and I'll take another cup of that black swill you call coffee, Louie, and one of those cherry Danishes, too."

Laura turned to see Linda Sturgis dragging a comb through her hair, then critically studying the results in a small hand mirror.

"Long night, huh?" the reporter asked as she dropped the mirror and comb into her oversized handbag.

"Longer than I expected," Laura said. "You don't know what's going on inside the house, do you?"

The woman shrugged. "I wish I did. But if I had to guess, I'd say that Sam's just being smart and waiting Crazy Janey out, not to mention praying that Ed Harrelson doesn't do something incredibly stupid."

"What do you mean?" Laura asked with a barely suppressed gulp.

"Oh, like tossing in a little tear gas canister or really going for the gusto with that precious SWAT team of his. He hasn't ruled that out, at least he hadn't when I last talked to him about fifteen minutes ago.''

"Oh, my God," Laura muttered, wondering if Sam knew what was going on outside, if he had any idea that all hell could break loose at any moment. It wasn't a good time to be fighting drowsiness, she decided, so she called up to the now deserted window of the snack truck. "That was two coffees, black."

Louie reappeared. "I'm making a fresh pot, ladies. It'll be done in just a second. Linda, I thought you said you were going to get around to interviewing me when there was a lull in the action." He aimed a thumb toward the house. "Hey, is this a lull, or what?"

The reporter looked at the house, then back at the man in the window, and grinned. "You know what, Louie? I'm so tired of talking to that idiot Harrelson that I'll do it. Just let me go find my cameraman." She took a step, then stopped to call back. "Oh, and Louie?"

"Yeah?"

"Didn't you mention something about free coffee and Danish for the duration."

"No problem, Linda. You got it," Louie said with a huge, gooey wink just before he produced a gray rag and began wiping down his counter and each plastic condiment bottle on it.

Laura cleared her throat. "Is that coffee done yet?"

"Oh, yeah. I forgot about you, Missy. Lemme check. That was two large black, right?"

"Right."

She stood there, staring at Janey's house, wishing she had X-ray vision and could see through the walls if only to reassure herself that Sam was still okay, thinking that a week ago she hadn't even known him and now, surprisingly, her future happiness somehow hinged on him.

"You better come out of this alive, Sam Zachary," she said softly.

"Laura?"

She whirled around at the sound of the male voice.

"Laura, doll. I saw you on the news." Artie's hand curved around her arm possessively. "I've been looking all over for you."

Chapter 13

It was the strangest, damnedest kiss Sam had ever experienced. Not only was his body eerily disengaged from the intimate act, but his mental focus was everywhere except on the woman he had successfully lured into his arms.

All the while they kissed, he kept one eye on the television screen, evaluating the scene outside the house and trying to anticipate Harrelson's next idiotic and possibly lethal move, and at the same time frantically searching his brain for remnants of his Marine Corps training.

The word *shimewaza* flitted through his mind, and long ago images of grimacing Marines with camouflage grease on their faces and no pity in their eyes. If done properly, Sam knew, a choke hold could render a person unconscious for several minutes. But the problem was that he'd never had an opponent who weighed less than a hundred seventy five pounds, the majority of which was muscle. And it went without saying that Captain Sam Zachary, USMC, had never been kissing the daylights out of the guy while attempting to subdue him.

Janey was built like her sister with bones as delicate as porcelain. She couldn't have weighed much over a hundred and ten, and her muscle tone left a lot to be desired. Right now, of course, every nerve in her little body was hot-wired with adrenaline. It was like kissing a time bomb covered with quivering flesh.

The Browning semi-automatic figured into Sam's equation, too, because even as Janey was melting like butter in his embrace, she stubbornly held onto the gun. At the moment, it was somewhere near the small of his back, undoubtedly pointed up toward his head. A bullet in the brain stem was definitely not the ideal ending to this scenario.

"Sam," Janey breathed against his mouth. "I've wanted this all my life. You know that, don't you? I've wanted *you* all my life."

"I'm here," he answered softly.

"I'll be better to you than Jenny ever was. I'll be better for you. She never loved you, Sam. She never..."

"Shh."

He shifted his right arm slightly higher, above her shoulder blade, and moved his right leg just a few inches forward preparatory to edging her off balance.

Somewhere among all his methodical calculations was the jarring notion that this should have felt like kissing Jenny, should have felt like having her back in his arms if only as a ghost. His heart, though, was as thoroughly disengaged as his body. Besides, it wasn't Jenny he wanted in his arms anymore. It was Laura. The thought almost made him forget everything else he was doing.

Forcing himself to focus on the television screen once more, he watched the newscam slowly pan away from Harrelson and his little knot of eager, camouflaged commandos, and swing out across the lawn toward the street where the snack truck was parked typically too close to the action. He could see that hustler, Louie, grinning like a snake oil salesman in the little awninged window from where he hawked his lousy coffee and greasy doughnuts, waving the cameraman toward him.

Dammit. Go back to Harrelson, Sam ordered silently. Turn the camera back on him. I need to know his every stupid move.

The camera paused momentarily, surprisingly, on Laura's pretty face, just long enough for Sam's heart to take a pronounced extra beat, and then the camera caught her turning all of a sudden to someone standing close, caught her stiffening, going rigid with fear as a hand clamped onto her arm.

Artie! All this TV coverage! Sam ought to have known.

"Sam. Love me. Love me. Love me. Take me away from here."

He had honest-to-God forgotten that his lips had been touching Janey's until she pulled away and whispered breathlessly against his ear.

"Love me, Sam. Take me away."

"I will, honey," he said, maneuvering her solidly back in front of him, easing his right forearm into the warm nook at the back of her neck, kissing her again, more forcefully this time while using his arm as a vise, pulling slowly and inexorably, putting what he hoped was the proper force on the nerves just below the base of Janey's delicate skull, and praying all the while that her finger wouldn't twitch on the trigger when she blacked out.

Laura had struggled so hard, so fiercely, that it had taken both Artie and his hulk of a bodyguard, Leo, to wrestle her away from the snack truck and get her into the back seat of the limousine. Nobody at the scene had noticed her struggle or even heard her screams because only seconds after Artie grabbed her by the arm, a shot had been fired inside the house that sent everybody—cops, reporters, curious on-lookers, even Louie—scrambling for cover.

Now, scrunched in the corner of her leather up-holstered prison, Laura wasn't even frightened. She was just frantic about Sam and so furious with rotten Artie that she wanted to strangle him with the thick gold chain he wore around his neck. The strangula-tion was going to have to wait, though. First she had to find out if Sam was okay. Oh, God. Please let him be okay, she prayed.

"I thought these things were supposed to have TVs," she snarled, gesturing around the dim confines of the limo.

"Well, sure." Artie gave her a decidedly wounded look as he gestured toward an envelope-sized screen mounted above the window that separated the vehi-cle's front and back seats. "It's got a full bar, too, doll. How about a drink?"

She hoped her glare would severely injure him. "I'd like to watch the news, if you don't mind."

"Sure, doll."

He let out an indulgent little sigh as he leaned to his left and flicked a switch. The minuscule screen overhead lit up, revealing Sheriff Harrelson's ferret-like face. Laura edged forward in the seat.

"Hey, doll, listen. I'm sorry about…"

"Shh," she hissed, her eyes intent on the televised scene in Janey's front yard. Where was Sam? Oh, God. Where was he? She didn't see him anywhere.

"But, listen…"

"Shh."

Linda Sturgis's face suddenly filled the little screen. "And so another possible tragedy has successfully been averted. The little girl, Samantha Sayles, was released without injury or incident, into the custody of her father, Wesley Gunther. Samantha's mother, Jane Sayles, is currently in the custody of the sheriff's department and being taken to Memorial Hospital where she will remain under observation as well as under arrest."

A wistful smile sketched across the reporter's lips. "As for former sheriff Sam Zachary, the man who brought an end to this bizarre drama, we don't have any more information at the present time. Our sources tell us that he was injured during a struggle for the Sayles woman's gun, but the nature or extent of those injuries isn't known. It's possible that he was also taken to Memorial Hospital, along with Jane Sayles. We'll have more details on our 6:00 a.m. Newsbreak. For now, that's all from here. This is Linda Sturgis, Channel Five News."

Laura sank back in the seat. "You can turn it off now, Artie," she said almost tonelessly.

Crouched behind a ragged forsythia bush two blocks west of Janey's house, Sam waited for Charlie to bring the Blazer around. If he didn't get away fast—from Harrelson's victory speech and the interminable questions of the press—he knew he might be too late to get to Laura before Artie did whatever Artie wanted to do in order to carve his initials on her.

He was hurt, but not enough to slow him down. The bullet, he was pretty sure, had zinged a little furrow across his side, just above his beltline. There wasn't time to worry about that now. He had to find Laura. If anything happened to her...

Charlie turned the corner, and Sam stood up to flag him down.

"I'm sorry, boss," was the first thing out of his mouth when he got out of the driver's seat. "She was getting coffee for us. I should've kept a better eye out."

"Don't worry about it," Sam said, hauling himself into the car.

"Hey, you're bleeding."

"Don't worry about that, either." Sam pulled the door closed.

"You need help?"

"Probably, but I'm headed into the city and you're on county time, Charlie. The last thing I want is any kind of jurisdictional hassle from Harrelson."

"Yeah. Well, you'll probably need this." The officer handed Sam's pistol in its shoulder holster through the window. Sam had taken it off prior to entering Janey's. "The sheriff was so busy brown-nosing the press that he didn't even see me take it."

"Thanks, Charlie." Sam shoved the gun under the seat, then put the truck in gear. "Gotta go."

"Wish I could help."

"Me, too."

* * *

"Well, what do you think of the place, doll?" Artie turned to Laura from the center of his leather and chrome and glass living room, his arms outstretched, a proud smile on his sleazy lips. "You like it?"

She hated it. She despised every stripped down, uncluttered, neutral, spare, antiseptic square inch of it. The off-white leather couches crouched on half an acre of wall-to-wall off-white carpet, and all of those walls were off-white, too. The only color Laura could detect was the green of the stalks of a vase of off-white silk lilies.

But even before she saw the apartment, while they were riding up seven stories in the elevator with Laura scrunched between rotten Artie and his trained gorilla, Leo, she knew she'd hate it.

"It's okay," she said, not willing to risk another black eye over a difference of opinion about decor.

"Okay?" Artie exclaimed. "This stuff set me back thirty thousand big ones, doll. It's a lot better than okay." He gestured to a far wall. "That's a genuine Eames chair. What do you think about that?"

Laura shrugged. All she cared about right now was Sam. Desperately. All she could think about was how she was going to get out of this horrible off-white wilderness and back to Sam.

Knowing Artie's tendency to violence when he didn't get his way, she decided she'd have to come up with a better strategy in order to escape. But what?

"How about a drink?" he asked. "I've got the best stocked bar in town. Whatever you want. A margarita. A Black Russian. The vodka's straight from Moscow. Ninety-nine bucks a quart."

"No, thanks. It's late. And I…"

Sudden inspiration struck.

"And I'm not feeling so well, Artie." Laura swayed slightly as she lifted her wrist to her temple, hoping she wasn't overdoing it. "Is there someplace I could lie down for a little while?"

He was beside her in an instant, the heavy musk of his cologne nearly toppling her. "I'll take you to my room," he said as he lifted her up in his arms and started across the wide expanse of carpet. "I was going to show it to you next, anyway."

I'll bet you were, Laura thought. She closed her eyes and pressed her head against his shoulder with a pitiful little moan. He wouldn't try anything with a defenseless sick woman, would he?

At the end of a long white track-lit hall, Artie pushed open a door and angled Laura through it.

"You're gonna love this, doll. Wait a sec. Lemme find the switch."

He leaned, Laura still in his arms, and snapped on a light.

"How about this?" he asked, jouncing her to attention.

If she really had been sick, she might have thrown up all over him. And not just from the jostling, but from the hideous, horrible room. It was black. Unrelieved, unadulterated, unparalleled black. The carpet. The walls. The furniture. Everything. It reminded Laura of a tomb. In contrast, the stark white living room seemed positively cheerful.

"You can put me down now," she said.

"Oh. Sure. Here." He walked toward an enormous bed and set her down on what felt like a leather bedspread. "Can I get you an aspirin or something?"

She lay back with her forearm draped wanly across her supposedly pale and feverish brow. "An aspirin would be good."

But since it would probably only take him half a minute to retrieve one, and Laura needed more time than that, she added, "Do you have any ice cream, Artie? It sounds silly, I guess, but sometimes that's the only thing that helps my headaches."

"Ice cream?" Artie appeared befuddled, at least as far as Laura could detect of his features in this sepulcher of a room.

"Yes." She turned on her side, drawing her knees up into a fetal position. "Strawberry seems to work the best."

"I dunno. I'll go look. You wait right here."

"I will."

"Want me to turn the light out, doll?"

"No. Please leave it on," she answered weakly.

"Okay. Stay there now. I'll be right back."

Laura counted to twenty to make sure Artie was gone before she sat up. Given the creep's penchant for physical violence, she'd already given up the notion of trying to escape on her own. There was no way she could outrun him. She'd have to outwit him, instead.

What she needed at the moment wasn't strawberry ice cream, but a telephone. Artie's turned out to be encased in a small ebony box on his black lacquer nightstand. But now that she had the phone, she didn't know who to call. If she called 9-1-1, what was she going to say? *Help, I'm being held prisoner in a black bedroom?*

Sam. She wanted to call Sam, and she didn't even know his phone number, plus he wasn't home even if she did. She wanted to hear his voice, to touch him and make sure he was all in one solid piece. She needed her Superman, not just to rescue her from this, but always. Somebody able to leap tall buildings and cook pizza from scratch, to blanch tomatoes and maybe even find the father she hadn't seen in over twenty years.

The father! Wait a minute. That was it. Not hers, but Artie's. Laura knew her landlord's phone number by heart and she knew he always worked late into the night. She punched the numbers quickly. If she couldn't call Superman to rescue her, maybe at least the Hammer could pound some sense into his son's thick, obnoxious head.

Sam didn't have a clue where Artie lived, but he knew how to find out. He used his left hand to push through the main doors of the Hammerman Building, trying to keep his right arm tight against his side to keep the bleeding at a slow leak.

One of the Hammer's goons jumped up from his seat near the door. "Hey, buddy, you can't come in here."

"I've got an appointment with the Hammer," Sam said, knowing it wasn't an outlandish statement. Art Hammerman was an insomniac who did most of his personal business at night. When Sam had worked for him, if they hadn't met in his office in the dead of night, it had been for breakfast at dawn.

"Give him a buzz," Sam said, pointing to a phone on a desk. "Tell him Sam Zachary's here."

The man's gaze slid from Sam's face to his shoulder holster, then continued down to his blood-soaked shirt. "Hey, how do I know you're on the level?"

"I guess the only way you're going to find out is by calling upstairs to the boss, Sherlock. Or do you want me to call and tell him there was nobody on the door when I came in?"

The goon's mouth flattened and his face turned a pale shade of mauve. Obviously fearing his employer's wrath far more than Sam's, he picked up the phone and a second later said, "There's a Sam Zachary here to see you, Mr. Hammerman."

He hung up the phone, glared at Sam, then angled his head toward the elevator. "The boss says to come on up."

On the fifth floor, Sam knocked on the carved double doors, but didn't wait for a reply to open them. The Hammer rose from the huge leather chair behind his desk and stuck out his hairy paw.

"Sam, good to see you. So, you thought about my offer and decided to come to work for me. That's good. That's great."

"I'm here about your son," Sam said, dispensing with the pleasantries. He didn't have the time or the inclination.

Art Hammerman rubbed his chest while the expression on his face turned from pleasure to disgust and then to something resembling horror as he noticed the blood on Sam's shirt. "Aw, damn," he muttered as he sank back into his big leather chair. "What'd the kid do now? Take a shot at you or something?"

"He abducted a woman against her will."

One of the Hammer's dark brows shot up. "What woman?"

"Laura McNeal, your tenant in the building on Russell Boulevard."

"That cute little blonde he was so crazy about?" He waved a hand dismissively. "He won't hurt her. The kid just kinda goes overboard where women are concerned. He's just fooling around."

Sam planted a fist on the desktop. "Well, this time he's fooling around with the woman I'm going to marry."

"Ah." He leaned back. "That's different, then. Have a seat, Sam."

"I'm kind of messed up," Sam said, glancing down at his side. "I wouldn't want to get..."

"Don't worry about it. I've got a woman works for me who can get any kinda stain out of anything. Sit."

Sam sat. Heavily. Wearily.

"Sheesh." The Hammer let out a breath. "I gotta say, Sam, I'm pretty relieved it wasn't my Artie who hit you, you know what I mean?"

"Yeah." It went without saying that if Artie had shot him, Sam would be looking to put the kid behind bars, and Big Daddy would have to do everything in his power to prevent that from happening.

"So, who did?" the Hammer asked.

"It was an accident. There was a hostage situation..."

"Oh yeah. I caught some of that on TV. That was you, huh?"

Sam nodded. "This woman. She came to me for help last week after Artie gave her a black eye. He

saw her on TV tonight and took her away against
her will. Any idea where they might be?''

''His apartment probably. He just got it done
over.'' Art Hammerman rolled his eyes. ''He likes
to show it off to the girls.''

''Where do I find it?''

Before the Hammer could answer, the phone on
his desk gave a soft but insistent chirp. He picked it
up and uttered a gravelly ''Yeah? Who is it?'', then
listened for a moment while a grin worked its way
across his lips.

''Hang on a minute, will you?'' He handed the
receiver to Sam, saying, ''It's your cute little blonde.
Smart little cookie, too.''

Waiting for Sam was interminable. Laura ate three
bowls of Chocolate Ripple ice cream, allowing each
one to melt to the consistency of cream soup, before
asking Artie for another.

''How do you stay so skinny?'' he'd asked in un-
disguised awe when he handed her the third helping
along with several napkins to spare the white sofa
and carpet.

She told him she had a fast metabolism, but wasn't
sure he even heard because he was already pointing
out another facet of the room's decor, droning on at
length about the genuine Chinese silk drapes and the
number of silk worms who gave up their lives in the
process, and of course not failing to mention their
staggering cost.

If he weren't such a creep, Laura might almost
have felt sorry for him. Artie wasn't a thug at heart.
He was just a lonely guy in search of somebody to

share his bizarre existence, and, having learned at his father's knee, the only way he knew to do it was by force.

On the phone Sam had told her to stay right here and to pretend that everything was all right, that he'd be here in less than half an hour. He had assured her over and over again that he was okay, but she didn't know whether to believe him or not. And now she was worried about what would happen when Sam arrived. Artie undoubtedly had a gun somewhere, and Leo the Gorilla always wore his in a little hand-tooled holster on his belt.

"All done with that?" Artie reached out for her bowl of Chocolate Ripple soup.

"Not quite." Laura was slurping up another spoonful just as the doorbell chimed the first six notes of "Some Enchanted Evening." She swallowed the ice cream then held her breath.

Leo appeared out of nowhere, a big blob of color in the stark white room. "I'll check it out, Artie," he mumbled on his way to the door.

Now, in addition to holding her breath, Laura closed her eyes. Be careful, Sam. The doorbell chimed again. Please be careful, Sam.

"Hey! How're you doing, boss?" Leo said.

"Great." There was no mistaking the Hammer's Godfather voice. "Take a hike, Leo."

Laura opened her eyes in time to see Leo shamble out and Art Hammerman stride in. Where was Sam? The question was almost to her lips when Artie exclaimed a startled, "Hey, Pop! What're you doing here?"

"I came to see the place," the Hammer said, easing into the room.

"It's after three in the morning, Pop."

"Yeah, well, you know, I figured it was about time, kid. You've been asking me to stop by and I was always too busy with this or that. So, now I'm not busy. Here I am." He looked around. "This is it, huh? This is your place?"

"This is it." The smile on rotten Artie's face was so full of pride and pleasure and filial adoration that Laura stopped hating him for two or three seconds. "Come on, Pop," Artie said. "Lemme show you around."

"Sure. That'd be great, kid." The Hammer was standing close to Laura's seat on the couch. He leaned a bit closer to her and lowered his voice to a rough whisper. "Sam's waiting for you downstairs, Blondie. You go on, now. And listen, you probably oughta take him straight to a hospital."

Laura was on her feet in an instant. She glanced in Artie's direction, uncertain of his reaction, but he didn't even seem aware of her presence now that his father had arrived. She started toward the door, but Art Hammerman delayed her with a hand on her arm.

"Don't worry about the kid here anymore, okay? You go on and have a happy life. You and Sam. And tell him I said that job offer still stands."

Laura couldn't help herself. She threw hers arms around the Hammer's neck and gave him a great big kiss on the cheek.

"Thank you," she whispered.

Then she made a beeline for the door. On her way out, she could hear Artie's excited voice.

"So, what do you think, Pop? Jeez, I'm glad you're here. You like it?"

"Yeah. It's nice, kid. It's real nice," the Hammer murmured. "It's very...well...white."

Chapter 14

Down on the street, Sam checked his watch and decided he'd give the Hammer five more minutes to bring this off before going in himself. The bodybuilder, presumably Artie's muscle, had already come out, pitched Sam a dark and suspicious glare, then shrugged and walked down the street. It was Laura's turn now. Where the hell was she?

He looked up at the lights on the penthouse floor, back at his watch, then fixed his gaze on the apartment building's door, practically willing it to open. Never in his life had he been unable to draw on a deep reservoir of patience. Waiting came naturally to him. Waiting for Jenny to say yes. Waiting for stray husbands to sneak out of hotels or for missing people to pick up mail at a post office box.

This was different, though. He felt as if he were dead, and he was waiting for his life to resume again. With Laura.

He'd had ample time on his drive to the Hammerman Building to consider some of the things that Janey had said about Jenny.

You went around with your head stuck in the sand for years, Sam. How could you have been such a fool? She was only using you. Good old strong dependable Sam.

At some level, he'd probably been aware of that, especially in their final years. But he'd made a commitment to Jenny. And, all in all, it wasn't such a terrible way to be used.

She was married to her music. She never wanted a home or a husband or kids.

He probably knew that, too. It just wasn't in his nature to let go.

Do you know what she used to call you behind your back? The Rube. Jenny's favorite name for you was Reuben Strongheart.

Even though Janey had been teetering on the edge of psychosis tonight, Sam believed every word she said. In his heart, he'd always known that about Jenny. But from kindergarten on, he just hadn't known how to let go.

The apartment building's door swung open, and Laura stepped out onto the sidewalk looking like an angel, momentarily confused by earth. She looked up the street, then back in his direction. Her feet hardly touched the pavement as she came flying into his arms.

"Oh, Sam. Are you all right? They said on the news..."

"Shh. I'm fine. What about you? If that guy so much as touched you..."

"No. He didn't. He didn't even try."

"That's good because I really wasn't looking forward to rearranging his face."

Laura stepped back, her worried gaze searching his face. "The Hammer said something about getting you to a hospital."

He turned slightly, gesturing to his side. "It's just a scratch, but..."

"A scratch!" Her eyes got huge. "Memorial Hospital isn't too far from here. Get in the truck, mister. Now."

"Whoa. Wait a minute. Memorial Hospital is where they took Janey. There's probably still half a dozen reporters lurking there, and I'm really not in the mood for the press right now. Why don't we just stop at the ER at Summit County on our way home?"

"You sure you'll be all right driving that far? It looks like you've lost a gallon of blood, Sam."

"Not quite, but if it'll make you feel better, you can drive. How's that?" He dug in his pocket for the keys and handed them over.

"Well, okay." She managed a little grin. "Do I get to speed and pick up a police escort along the way?"

Sam laughed. "I sincerely hope not."

"You're no fun," she said, climbing behind the wheel.

Sam's head was canted back against the seat and his eyes were closed, but he still had an uncanny ability to tell Laura which way to turn at each intersection. Thank heavens, she thought, otherwise she would have been driving in circles for the past half hour while Sam bled to death in the passenger seat.

"Take a left at the next light," he said. "The hospital's about two miles down the road."

"Okay." She flipped on the directional signal, determined to press the accelerator to the floor those next few miles because of the worry she detected in his voice. Waiting for the green light, she glanced to her right to find her Superman looking more grim than he had only moments before. There was a fine sheen of perspiration on his forehead. "Hang on, tough guy. We're almost there."

"Great."

From the note of doom in his voice, it suddenly dawned on Laura that Sam wasn't half as concerned about the loss of blood or the bullet wound as he was about what undoubtedly awaited him in one of those little curtained-off cubicles in the ER. A needle! Surely any bullet wound, no matter how superficial, would require a tetanus shot.

She almost laughed. Her hero, the man who had taken on the Devil's Own, a crazed woman with a gun, and the major players in the city's underworld in the past few days, was a quivering wreck at the mere thought of a hypodermic needle. She didn't know whether to tease him or offer sympathy or ignore his plight altogether. All she really knew was that she adored him.

"Nervous?" she asked, testing the waters.

"Who, me?" He sat up a little straighter. "Nah."

"That's good." She turned the Blazer into the hospital parking lot, found a spot close to the door, and pulled in. "Well, we're here."

"Yeah. Okay." He reached for the door handle, then drew back his hand. "You know, why waste their time? This really isn't anything more than a scratch. It doesn't even hurt anymore. Honest to God. Let's just go home and slap a Band-Aid on.''

Laura bit her lip to keep from grinning. ''I don't think so, Sam. Let's go.''

''Yeah. Okay.''

He wrenched the door open. Laura grabbed the keys and sprinted around the Blazer to help him ease out.

''Can you walk okay?'' she asked.

''Oh, yeah. Sure.'' He took a hesitant step toward the brightly lit entrance to the ER, then reached out his hand to take hers. A rueful little curse broke from his lips. ''This is so damned humiliating.''

''I know, sweetheart.'' Laura squeezed his clammy hand. ''But this time it's going to be a piece of cake.''

''How do you know that?''

She smiled mysteriously. ''Because I have a plan.''

Sam's smile was a little wobbly. ''Let me guess. You're going to give me a blindfold, right?''

''Nope. Something much better. Trust me.''

When they walked through the doors of the ER, Sam was greeted with a quick burst of applause that brought forth a muted curse only Laura could hear. Luther, the aide, sauntered up, his hand raised in a high five.

''Yo, Sam. My man.''

Sam returned the gesture without enthusiasm.

''We watched your little party on the tube in the lounge, man. Had a little action going over who'd prevail, the new sheriff with his fancy SWAT team or ol' Cool Hand Sammy.''

''Who'd you put your money on?'' Sam asked.

Luther grinned as he produced a wad of bills from the pocket of his green scrubs. "You're my main man, man. What can I say?" His gaze cut to Sam's side and his expression sobered. "Sorry about that. We'll have you out of here in no time."

"They need you in the OR, Luther," Norma Jefferson snapped, whirling the young man by his shoulders and giving him a shove down the corridor before she turned her cool, efficient gaze back to Sam. "You should have come in sooner, Sam."

"Well, I'm here now, Norma," he said.

"Room Number Two." She jabbed her ballpoint pen toward the curtained-off cubicle. "Janey's friend can take a seat in the waiting room."

"I'd rather not," Laura said, linking her arm through Sam's, taking the full brunt of the charge nurse's glare.

"I'm sorry, but you'll…"

"She's *my* friend, Norma," Sam snapped, then softened his tone considerably when he added, "Gimme a break here, will you? I need all the moral support I can get."

The woman rolled her eyes and sighed. "All right. Go in there and take off your jeans. Not your shirt, though. I'm going to cut that off around the wound, then we'll see what needs to be done. Give a yell when you're ready."

Sam gave Laura's arm a squeeze before he disappeared through the curtains.

"This isn't a good time to slap Sam with a big I-told-you-so about Janey Sayles," the woman said quietly, pausing just long enough to give a brisk cluck of her tongue, "so I'll let you have it, instead.

Why the hell didn't somebody do something before she went over the edge?''

"I told him so, too," Laura said. "I think Sam's just too kind-hearted to say no or goodbye. He didn't want to hurt her."

"Well, at least she'll be getting some help now."

"Norma," Sam called. "Let's get this over with."

The nurse held the curtain back for Laura, clucked her tongue again, and said, "After you."

Sam shifted onto his side on the narrow examining table, and cocked his arm to brace his head.

"I feel like a slab of meat," he said, trying his best to sound cavalier while his shirt was being scissored away, failing dismally because neither Laura nor Norma laughed in response. "What's the verdict, Norma?"

"She got you pretty good. My God, Sam. Janey must've been standing only a couple inches away when she pulled the trigger. I'm going to have to clean the gunpowder and bits of fabric out of here, then I'll debride the wound so it'll heal properly, without a lot of ragged edges."

"Okay," he said. "Go ahead."

He fashioned a tough-guy grin for Laura who was perched on a metal stool directly in front of him. Her black eye was almost gone, but now there were dark smudges of exhaustion beneath both eyes. He'd put her through a hell of a wringer tonight, that was for sure. All he wanted to do now was take her home and tuck her safely, warmly in bed beside him.

"Tired?" he asked softly.

Her pretty face brightened for his benefit, and she shook her head.

"We'll be out of here in no time," he said.

"I don't want to be the one to spoil your plans, Sam," Norma said from behind him, "but this is going to take more than a few minutes." Then she raised her voice. "Cindy, I want to run an antibiotic IV. One gram of Ancef. Will you bring it in Two, please?"

Sam swallowed so loud he didn't hear whatever else Nurse Ratchet was saying. Laura's pretty face blurred for a moment. Then Cindy suddenly appeared, grinning like a jack-o-lantern, holding a little plastic bag with seventeen miles of tubing attached to it. Somewhere in there, Sam was certain, there was a foot long needle.

He was going to pass out.

"You people are sadists," he groaned.

"I need your left arm, Sam," Norma said sternly. Her voice sounded like it was coming from deep inside a cave. A witches' cavern full of bats and lizards. "Sam, work with me now, okay? Just relax your arm, for heaven's sake."

He couldn't, dammit.

"Hey." Laura scooted toward him on her metal stool. Her face was level with his, so close that all she had to do was whisper. "I've been wondering, Sam. Do you think it's possible to fall in love in just a few days? I mean really, deeply, head over heelsy in love?"

"Do I...?" His focus narrowed on her blue, blue eyes and the tiny gold speckles in them. "Why do you ask?"

"Well..." She scooted closer so her nose was almost in contact with his and her breath warm on his lips when she continued. "I'm asking because I'm pretty sure I've fallen really, deeply, head over heelsy in love with you."

"Yeah?" His mouth twitched in something comparable to a smile.

"Yeah," she purred, her lips just brushing his. "I must be nuts, huh?"

"That would make two of us."

"Yeah?" She leaned even closer, her soft mouth pressing against his for a long, sweet moment, her tongue teasing and tantalizing him. "So, you think maybe we're both sharing the same sexy delusion?"

"Could be." Sam was fairly certain he was delusional because of the lingering taste of Chocolate Ripple ice cream on his lips.

"What do you think we should do about it?" she whispered. "I mean other than spend at least twelve out of every twenty-four hours in bed, making incredible love for the next forty or fifty years?"

Sam could feel a dopey smile take possession of his mouth. That had to be the reason he couldn't quite form the words to match the incredible images in his brain. His eyelids felt like freshly poured concrete, but he managed to blink once—for yes—hoping Laura would get the message.

"I love you, Sam."

He sighed all the way to the soles of his feet.

Luther's voice floated somewhere above him. "All right, mama. You go, girl."

Then Laura. "He's awfully relaxed."

Then Norma, the sadist. "You did a nice job distracting him. Our good friend, Mr. Valium did the rest. I'll be done here in just a few minutes. Oh, and by the way, I hope you meant what you said because this is one guy who really deserves to be loved. If you didn't mean it, I hope you never show your face in my ER again.''

A few hours later, when they left the ER, Sam was looking a lot less like Superman than the Jolly Green Giant in the hospital scrubs that Norma had given him to replace his blood-stained clothes.

Laura jingled the truck keys in her hand as they walked across the parking lot, trying to stifle the yawns that kept creeping up on her. The eastern sky was already pale shades of pink and amethyst, promising a lovely day after their long, terrible night. She was exhausted. Sam, on the other hand, after his little Valium snooze, seemed bright-eyed and chock-full of ungodly energy. She swore she could hear him whistling as he trailed along behind.

One of the yawns suddenly overtook her. ''Oh, Lord,'' she sighed. ''I can't wait to get into bed.''

The next thing she knew, Sam overtook her, wrapping his arms around her from behind. ''I can't wait to get you there. Tell me you meant every word you said earlier in the ER, Laura. Tell me it wasn't just a diversionary tactic.''

She leaned her head back on his shoulder. ''You mean the part about making love for twelve out of every twenty-four hours?''

''That, too.'' He chuckled, his breath warm at her ear. ''But I was thinking more about the 'I love you, Sam' part. The 'how is this possible in such a short time' part.''

''Oh, that.''

In all honesty, Laura thought that Sam had either forgotten what she'd said to distract him from the dreaded hypodermic needle, or that her words had never actually registered on his woozy brain. She felt embarrassed now, and foolish for having spoken those words. It *was* nuts to believe that people fell in love that fast. Especially two people so determined not to do it.

"Well?" Sam asked.

"Well, what?"

"Did you mean it? Or were you just making emergency room conversation?"

Laura swallowed hard. The words that had come to her so easily an hour ago seemed impossible to express. She'd meant them with all her heart, but right now she wished she hadn't said them. "What I said was it's crazy to think that it...love...you know...could happen so fast."

With his arms still around her, Sam rested his chin on the top of her head. "Fast. Slow. What's the difference, Laura, as long as it happens?"

The sun was visible now, a brilliant orange ball climbing over the tree line miles away to the east. A brand new day. So full of promise. If only she could believe...

"Are you saying you love me, Sam?"

"I was working up to it." He laughed softly. "Yeah. I'm saying I love you, Laura. Probably from the minute you walked into my office."

He sounded so certain. He felt so warm, so solid, so permanent. Oh, God. It was going to tear her heart right out of her chest when he left her.

Because, all of her shining hopes and happy dreams and heartfelt wishes aside, that was the one thing Laura knew she could count on. Men leaving.

* * *

Sam was glad to see the kitchen window had been boarded up. He led Laura through the back door and across the kitchen where their feet scrunched on broken glass.

"I'm too beat to clean this up right now," he said, continuing into the hallway and toward the stairs.

"I'll help you," Laura said. "Aw, Sam. First the mirror in the living room, and now the window. It's all my fault, too. I must be a jinx. All this broken stuff."

"Hey."

She was on the first step, so when he turned her around their faces were level. He cradled her face in both hands, smoothing his thumbs over her cheeks. "I think it was time for a few things to get broken around here. Time for me to break with the past and start looking toward the future. And if that's all your fault, sweetheart, then I'm very grateful."

Leaning to kiss the tip of her nose, Sam could see a warm shimmer of tears in Laura's eyes.

"I'm going to love loving you, Sam," she whispered. "No matter how long it lasts, I'm going to love every minute of it."

A tear broke loose from the corner of her eye, and Sam thumbed it away, wishing there were some way to reassure her of his constancy, knowing that only time would do that.

"Know what I'm going to say to you on our fiftieth wedding anniversary?" he asked.

A surprised little laugh broke from her throat. "I can't imagine."

"I'm going to say 'I told you so.'"

Her smile warmed his heart even though it con-

tained a hint of wariness. Sam knew she didn't believe him. He decided he'd have to do something else
to convince her. Fifty years was far too long to wait
for the security she deserved.

Chapter 15

When they awoke together in the late afternoon after the Janey and Artie debacle, the first thing Sam muttered was a mournful, "We need a bigger bed."

Laura snuggled closer to him, careful not to disrupt the gauze dressing taped to his side, pressing her knees into the backs of his, while stifling a giggle. "A bigger bed? Oh, I don't know, Sam. I kind of like sleeping in the bottom bunk. It reminds me of summer camp."

"You went to summer camp?" he asked.

"Yes. Twice as a matter of fact. Why do you sound so surprised?"

Sam chuckled. "Outside?"

"Very funny." Her foot connected solidly with his calf. "There weren't any wolf spiders on the premises. Or coyotes."

He was quiet a moment. "You know, we don't have to stay here if you don't want, Laura."

"Are you kidding me? I adore this place!" she exclaimed. "Well, the inside, anyway. Besides, you've lived here all your life, Sam. I wouldn't change that."

She levered up on an elbow and gazed over Sam's shoulder, taking in the details of his time-warped room—the faded felt pennants on the walls, the dusty trophies and tattered textbooks, all the old memories. One old memory in particular caught her eye—Jenny Sayles, smiling out from her shiny silver frame.

The little stitch of jealousy that pulled tight inside her wasn't something Laura was proud of. She thought of her mother suddenly, ripping up individual photographs of her father and snipping him out of every family group. Sam and Jenny Sayles had been together for a long, long time. Laura supposed she could make peace with the portrait, given ample time.

"I love being here with you, Sam, and I know that losing Jenny was very painful for you," she said, reaching up and combing her fingers through his hair, letting her fingertips play over the creases at the corners of his eye and the soft whiskers on his cheeks.

"I forgot the damned picture," he snapped. He wrenched upright and reached for the bottom half of the hospital scrubs he'd taken off several hours before, cursing softly as he put them on. "Sorry, honey. I meant to get rid of it as soon as we got home this morning."

Laura's first inclination was to lie and to cheerfully reassure him that the photograph didn't bother her at all. Not one bit. Why, she hardly even noticed it. Her second inclination, which she followed, was to say nothing. She watched Sam practically stalk across the room, pick up the frame and pull the photo roughly from beneath the glass.

"Don't rip it!" The words came out before Laura even realized they were on her tongue.

He looked at her, startled. "What?"

"I said don't rip it. Please." Laura sat up, bunching the bed covers around herself. "Just put it away someplace, Sam. She meant so much to you for such a long time. It just wouldn't be right, tearing it up."

"Maybe you're right," he murmured, looking down at the picture in his hands, then folding it crisply and jamming it in a drawer before looking back at Laura. The expression on his face wavered momentarily between sadness and profound relief.

The same emotions played in his voice when he said, "I didn't really have a chance to tell you last night, but Janey said some things that... Well, hell, basically what she said was that I'd been a total jerk most of my life because Jenny never cared. Not about me, anyway."

He lifted his shoulders in a helpless shrug while a mournful little grin flickered across his lips. "I haven't decided yet which is worse—being a jerk or wasting a quarter of a century's worth of affection on a woman who never had any intention of making a life with me."

"Oh, Sam, honey."

Laura almost wished Jenny Sayles were still alive so she could have the exquisite pleasure of strangling her with her own tiara. She hated the woman. Worse, she hated seeing Sam so deeply hurt. She reached out her arms to him, hoping somehow to soften the blow he'd taken. "You shouldn't believe any of that.

I mean, considering Janey's condition and all. She was probably just making it all up."

"No." He shook his head. "Janey was finally telling the truth for once in her life. The funny thing is, I think on some level I knew it all along."

He lowered himself onto the bunk beside her, sighing as Laura's arms folded around his chest. He bent his head against hers and said, "Hell of a thing for a man to have to admit about himself—that what he always considered loyalty and faithfulness was nothing more than sheer stupidity and stubbornness."

"How could she not have loved you?" Laura whispered, her lips pressing against his shoulder. "You're everything good, Sam. Jenny was a fool for not seeing that."

Sam laughed softly. "Ah, well, kiddo, it looks as if you and I are in nearly the same boat now. We've got a lot more in common than either one of us realized."

"What do you mean?"

"I mean we're both starting from scratch, in a way. Look at us. You lost all your worldly goods in a fire, and I've just been burnt out of about twenty-five years worth of memories."

"So, we'll make new ones, Sam," Laura said, tightening her embrace. "Better ones. I promise you."

Sam never actually proposed. Not in the traditional bended knee, diamond-ring-in-the-blue-velvet-box sort of way. Not in so many words.

He didn't know how to put the words together right, and somewhere deep inside, he was afraid—coward that he was—that if he actually asked her,

Laura's answer would be no. But during the next few weeks, he made it absolutely clear that he intended to marry her.

He bought a bigger bed. Not a total coward, he surprised Laura with one he saw in the window of an antique store a few blocks from his office. A big, sexy brass bed and a rose-colored mattress that guaranteed a decade of perfect sleep.

"See that," he told her, pointing out the printed tag stitched to the underside of the mattress. "That's a ten year commitment. Just for starters. If you want, I'll sign my name right there in indelible ink."

She'd laughed at that, but there was something in her eyes that said she still didn't believe their relationship would outlast the warranty. Men left her. That was what was printed indelibly on her heart. There was nothing Sam could say to convince her otherwise. He knew he'd have to show her. Soon.

If he'd learned one thing from Jenny, it was that life was too short and love was too precious to waste. Just as he needed to give one hundred percent of his love and loyalty to Laura, he required the same from her in return. And, by God, he wasn't going to wait fifty years for that 'I told you so.'

On the day Sam planned to file for the sheriff's election, Laura edged delicately out of the big brass bed and slinked down to the kitchen, determined to prepare a fabulous breakfast for him. Well, semi-fabulous. As in freshly thawed orange juice, plain everyday scrambled eggs, easy-to-brown link sausages, and unburnt—she hoped!—whole wheat toast.

Sam, bless his heart, went back for seconds, then thirds.

"You're sweet, Sam, but you really don't have to make yourself sick just to prove it's edible," Laura said as she was sopping up the last runny bit of egg with a corner of very dark—okay, burnt—toast.

"If I weren't due at the courthouse in half an hour," he said, glancing at the clock on the wall, "I'd be tempted to go back for fourths."

Laura stared at the yellow and black morsel in her fingertips for a moment, then dropped it back onto her plate.

"Okay. Okay. I'll take cooking lessons." She flung her hands up in surrender. "There. I've said it. I'll sign up for a class or something this week."

Sam arched a wicked eyebrow. "That sounds perilously close to optimism to me, Miss McNeal. As if you're actually beginning to believe you'll have people to cook for in the coming years." He grinned. "Me. A couple of rug rats, maybe. Even, heaven help you, grandkids."

"Don't press your luck, my love. It's just that you'll be working longer hours after the election and I don't want to go to jail for poisoning the sheriff."

"Speaking of the election," he said, "how about coming to the courthouse with me? I thought maybe we could get a marriage license...you know...just in case."

"Sam," she said softly.

Oh, God. He was the sweetest, most generous, strongest and sexiest man in the entire world. He had even risked salmonella and God knows what else this morning in order to please her. She was the luckiest woman alive. Why couldn't she just relax and accept his gift of love? Why couldn't she just say yes?

He was sitting there, his empty plate on the table

before him, his gaze fastened so intently on her face, his expression so…so, worried. No. More than that. Scared! So damned scared.

It nearly broke her heart.

"Okay," she said, almost breezily, as if there'd never been a single doubt or any hesitation whatsoever in her mind. As if she naturally assumed he'd stick around forever.

"Let's get the license. Just in case."

His handsome features kind of melted with relief. "Great. We'll drop by the clerk's office and get it, then."

"Fine." Laura gave a tiny shrug, more to ease the sudden, terrible tension in her shoulders than to communicate indifference. "Let's do it. Besides, there's no law that says once we've got the license that we have to use it, right?"

"No," he said with a shake of his head. "At least, none that I know of. And I'm pretty familiar with all the laws in the county."

"Okay, then."

"Okay."

Laura cleared her throat. "Just in case."

"Right. No big deal. Just in case."

The big deal, as it turned out, wasn't getting the marriage license or even when Sam fainted during the subsequent blood test. The big deal—the mother of all big deals, in fact—was the following week when Laura made a sudden and unprecedented trip to the grocery store and came home with a gallon of milk, a roll of mints, and a do-it-yourself pregnancy test.

Sam stared at the items as she took them from the

paper bag. Then he swallowed, much too audibly he thought for a guy who was six three, weighed in at over two hundred pounds, and was about to resume wearing a badge and a .357 Magnum on a daily basis. Then he grinned.

"What were these?" he asked, laughing as he pointed to the plastic milk jug and the candy on the kitchen table. "A diversionary tactic for the checkout lady?"

"Not funny," she said, aiming a glare right between his eyes. "I think we're in big trouble, Sam. This could well be the case we were talking about when we said 'Just in case.'"

"I think it's the best news I've ever had in my life, Laura." He slipped his arms around her, absorbing her brief, half-hearted struggle. "I love you so much," he whispered. "This is perfect."

"I love you, too," she said on a long sigh. "But I'm not so sure this is perfect."

He hugged her tighter. "Yes, it is. Let's go take the test. Come on. Right now."

"I sort of thought I'd wait." Her voice wobbled and she shrugged weakly against him. "You know. Just take my time reading the instructions. Contemplate the box a little while. That kind of thing."

"Nope." He picked her up, then reached for the test kit and jammed it in her hand. "Here. You can read the instructions on our way up the stairs."

After nudging Laura into the bathroom and closing the door, Sam settled on the top step, leaning against the wall with his arms crossed and one leg cocked, trying to look casual even as he was reminding himself to breathe every now and then. He checked his watch about every forty-five seconds, unsure how long these things took.

Still, he had no doubt about the outcome. Laura was pregnant. He was sure. The gods of happiness wouldn't lift a man this high if they only meant to drag him down. Would they? Even closing his eyes did nothing to erase what felt like the goofiest of grins from his lips.

A baby! A delicate little girl with Laura's soft blond hair and huge blue eyes. A little girl who'd play endless dress up in her mother's crazy clothes and who'd learn early on to laugh at thunder and lightning. Or a brown-haired boy, a sweet, good-natured doofus who'd take decades to grow into his inherited big hands and feet.

Ah, God. A baby. This changed everything.

Or not.

Sam's grin evaporated. He opened his eyes and shoved off the wall. It didn't change a thing as far as Laura's fear of abandonment was concerned. Hell. It might even make it worse since she knew better than anyone that a man could just as easily walk out on a woman and a child.

Damn you, Oliver McNeal. I haven't found you for her yet, but I will if it's the last thing I ever do. I'll find you and somehow I'll make you fix what you broke all those years ago.

When Officer Travis knocked on the back door, Laura immediately knew it was somewhere between four and four-thirty because for the past three weeks he'd knocked on the back door every single after-noon between four and four-thirty. Sam had asked him to check on her ever since the plus sign appeared on the test stick. Of course, if Sam was as concerned about her condition as he claimed to be, Laura thought that he could have spent a little more time at home, himself, instead of making poor Charlie do it.

Ever since finding out she was pregnant, Sam had all but disappeared. He said he was winding up cases at his office prior to his certain reelection as sheriff. Laura wasn't so sure. Her worst fear was that he was getting cold feet now that their ''just in case'' had materialized in the form of a baby.

"Come on in, Charlie," she called. "I'm glad you're here. I need a guinea pig."

"You need a what?" he asked, pulling open the screen door, then sloughing off his cap as he stepped into the kitchen.

"A guinea pig. I'm making chili for the very first time. From scratch!" She dipped a clean spoon into the pot on the back burner, scooped up some of the chunky, simmering, bright red concoction, and passed it to the officer. "See what you think. Be careful, though. It's hot."

"Looks great," he said, smiling as he blew a few cooling breaths at the rising steam before he inserted the spoon and its contents in his mouth. "Mmm."

Laura held her breath.

When she hadn't been able to find a cooking class in which to enroll, she'd picked up a copy of a gourmet magazine instead. Most of the recipes were daunting if not downright terrifying, with ingredients like duck fat and fennel and leeks. But the recipe for chili seemed easy enough, and she'd spent the morning happily chopping onions and green peppers and garlic, humming even, and so in hopes of pleasing Sam with her newfound expertise.

But as she watched, Charlie's expression of sheer, even heavenly pleasure altered somewhat to mild distress, and then, a few seconds later, it mutated to pure horror. He grimaced. His eyes bulged out and his hand jerked up to his collar. Laura thought he was teasing her, and she didn't much appreciate it when he made a horrible strangling sound deep in his throat.

"What?" she asked, glaring at him.

"Water!"

"Water?"

"Water!!"

Charlie's hands flailed in the direction of the sink, which he apparently couldn't see at the moment because of the tears in his eyes. Oh, God. He wasn't kidding. She grabbed a glass and filled it from the tap. After Charlie gulped down all sixteen ounces, he gestured for more.

While he drank the second glass, Laura poked a spoon in the chili pot and tasted it for herself. It wasn't so bad, she thought, just before the top of her head exploded and flames shot out of her eyes.

Not bothering with a glass, she stuck her head under the faucet and turned the water on full blast.

"What did I do wrong?" she moaned after she finally came up for air.

"Dunno," Charlie said, his voice sounding slightly sandpapery, as if his vocal chords had been shredded. "How much chili powder did you use?"

"Only what the recipe called for. A cup, I think. Let me check."

Laura snatched the magazine off the counter and

ran a finger down the page, ticking off the ingredients.

"Oh," she murmured. "Oh, damn." She didn't know whether she wanted to cry or to take a sledgehammer to the stove. "It was supposed to be two tablespoons of chili powder and one cup of chopped green pepper. I think I got them mixed up."

"Well…" Charlie shrugged and said, "I can definitely see how that could happen." He slapped his cap on his head. "I'd better be going, Laura. I'll see you tomorrow."

"Okay," she sighed, turning the burner off under her hellacious brew. "See you tomorrow, Charlie."

She had just crammed the last of it into the garbage disposal when Sam called from his office to announce that not only would he not be home for dinner, but not for breakfast either since he was about to catch a plane for Chicago.

"Why?" Laura asked, trying not to sound too disappointed or too upset by his continuing absences.

"I need to pull together a few loose ends on one of my cases," he said.

"Oh."

She could hear him sigh one of those beleaguered and all too familiar, when-will-you-trust-me sighs. But how could she? He was already leaving her. It just happened to be in bits and pieces rather than the ultimate farewell.

"Will you be all right alone tonight?" he asked. "Want me to call Charlie and…?"

"Don't be silly, Sam. I'll be fine." *Peachy. Alone. Again. Now there's a surprise.*

Laura tried to lighten her voice. "Hey, you're going to miss a great dinner. I made chili today."

"No kidding? Aw, honey, I'm sorry. This just kind of came up out of the blue."

"That's okay."

"Save some for me, will you?"

"Sure." *Might as well make up another vat of it tomorrow. What else is there to do while I wait for the axe to fall?*

"The plane's boarding, sweetheart. Gotta go. I'll call you later from Chicago."

"Okay. Have a good trip."

"I love you, Laura."

"I love you, too, Sam. Bye."

"Goodbye again," she whispered after hanging up. "I just didn't think it would be quite so soon."

In window seat 20-C, Sam buckled his seat belt, then leaned back his head and closed his eyes. It hadn't taken a private investigator to detect the sadness and insecurity in Laura's voice, or the subtext of her every word, her eternal *Go ahead. Leave. Everybody does. Why should you be any different?*

Hell. If this Oliver McNeal in Chicago didn't pan out, Sam didn't know what he was going to do. He'd just about exhausted the few leads that he'd gleaned from Laura during casual conversations. Her father's name, his approximate age, a remembered reference to an unnamed aircraft carrier.

Unbeknownst to Laura, Sam had spent the last three weeks trying to find the right man out of the dozens of names he'd turned up. He'd even taken a day trip to Omaha the previous week to meet with an Oliver McNeal who turned out to be not only the wrong age, but the wrong color as well.

But finding the man wasn't his biggest problem.

It was finding the reason he'd abandoned his little girl, and Sam could only do that in person, man-to-man, eye to eye. A letter or a phone call weren't going to tell him what he really needed to know, which was whether or not he might be reintroducing Laura to a man who might hurt her all over again.

He looked out the window while the plane hurtled down the runway. She made chili today! Ah, God. He couldn't wait to get home.

Chapter 16

When Charlie knocked on the door the next day, Laura looked at the clock on the stove, imagining she'd gone into a trance while stirring her second batch of chili and had somehow lost three hours. But that wasn't the case. It was just a little after one o'clock.

"Cooking again, huh?" the officer asked without a trace of sarcasm as he entered the kitchen. "Smells great."

"You're early today, Charlie."

"Sam asked me to pick you up and take you to the courthouse."

Laura dropped the spoon into the pot. "What?"

"He said to get you there by two-thirty or else."

"Why?" It was only now that she noticed a kind of silly smile perched on the officer's lips. "What in the world is this about?"

"Well…" The smile got even sillier. "A wedding,

I guess. He said to tell you to wear your wedding dress and to make sure you bring the license.''

She snapped off the heat under the pot. "Why didn't he call me himself?"

Charlie shrugged. "He tried, I guess, but there was no answer. Then he said he had to catch a plane, so I should come get you." He glanced at his watch. "We don't have all that much time, especially if you've got to get into a wedding dress."

"I don't *have* a wedding dress," she muttered. "This is ridiculous."

"All I know is Sam said he'd kick my butt all the way across the county if I didn't get you to Judge Randle's chambers on time. Look. Just put on any old dress, Laura, grab the license and let's go."

Laura stalked up the stairs, after proclaiming that she was only doing this to keep Charlie out of trouble, no way was she doing it for Sam, no way was she going to go through with a marriage to a man who spent more time away from home than in it, and no way was her baby going to be abandoned. If he or she didn't have a daddy to begin with, that was fine. That was perfect. Then there wouldn't be anybody to walk out on them. Ever.

She glared at the big brass bed that Sam had bought her, and hot tears began to well up in her eyes. Being with Sam was the most important thing in her life. She wanted to marry him. She wanted to cook his meals and have his children and share this bed with him forever.

"What is wrong with you?" she muttered. "Just put on a damned dress and go marry the man. Whatever happens. However long it lasts."

After she wiped her eyes, she raked her T-shirt over her head and wriggled out of her jeans.

"What damned dress?"

She still hadn't replaced the clothes she'd lost in the fire. There wasn't much incentive when she knew her size would be changing continually during the coming months. Briefly, she considered getting something from Sam's mother's closet, then decided she didn't want to get married looking matronly and reeking of White Shoulders.

Which left her with only one option.

Laura opened a dresser drawer and pulled out her little blue velvet dress. One thing was for sure. When Sam walked out on their marriage, at least he wouldn't ever forget their wedding day.

Sam paced back and forth in front of the county courthouse. He checked his watch for the ninetieth time since he and Oliver McNeal had deplaned, sprinted to Sam's Blazer in the parking lot, then broken more than a few speed limits between the airport and the courthouse.

He told Charlie two-thirty, didn't he? Dammit. It was now two-forty. Judge Randle had to be back on the bench at three. Worse, Oliver McNeal had to be back on a plane to Chicago at three forty-five in order to catch his six o'clock flight to Kuwait where the man was about to begin a two-year stint as a drilling consultant.

His heart sped up when he saw a squad car pull into the courthouse parking lot, but the tags didn't match Charlie's. He swore, loud enough to garner him an indignant *tsk* from an elderly woman several feet away.

"I'm getting married," he said by way of apology. "And my bride is fifteen minutes late."

She gave him another sharp little cluck of her tongue, then said, "You oughtn't marry her, if she's not worth waiting for."

"Oh, she's worth it. It's just that…"

Sam felt his mouth close helplessly. What could he say? It was way too complicated to explain. All he knew was that if Laura didn't get here in the next few minutes, his perfect plan was going to fall apart. She might still consent to marry him, but it wouldn't be the wedding he wanted to give her.

Charlie—God bless him!—roared around the corner and brought his cruiser to a screeching stop in front of the courthouse entrance. Sam sprinted forward to open the back door where Laura sat, arms crossed and head down, looking for all the world like someone who'd just been picked up for… prostitution!

She had it all on. The whole nine glitzy, glamorous yards. Better yet, the single, skimpy yard of blue velvet with the neckline down to there and the hem halfway up her gorgeous legs. The killer, rhinestone studded shoes. Even the tiny beaded bag barely big enough for a key and a Kleenex. Even as he fell head over heels in love all over again, Sam was sorely tempted to strangle her.

He stretched out his hand and helped her out of the seat. "Hurry, babe."

"Sorry we're late, boss," Charlie said.

"It's my fault, Sam," Laura said. "I dawdled. Don't blame Charlie."

"I don't have time to blame anybody." He propelled her toward the courthouse entrance, and called over his shoulder. "Step it up, will you, Charlie? We need a second witness."

"Sam! For heaven's sake, slow down. I can't walk that fast in these shoes."

He pushed through the door and headed toward the elevator, steering Laura through the crowded lobby and ignoring her repeated protests as well as the curious looks and assorted wolf whistles that followed them. At the elevator, he punched the up button and then gazed down at his bride.

"Did you bring the license?"

"Right here." She extracted it, folded and refolded until it was barely bigger than a postage stamp, from her purse. "Are you sure you want to do this in such a big rush, Sam? Maybe it's not such a great idea. Maybe we should wait. Maybe, you know, I should get the right kind of dress. This could be a jinx or something. Maybe..."

The elevator doors whooshed open and he moved her forward, gently but firmly.

Charlie slid through the doors just as they were closing.

"I had to leave the cruiser out front in that no parking zone, Sam. I hope it doesn't cost you too many votes." The officer dragged in a breath. "Did I hear you right? You want me to be a witness?"

"Yep."

Charlie grinned as he swept his hat off and ran his fingers through his hair. "Gee, thanks, Sam. I'm flattered. I really am. I'll be proud to stand up for you."

Laura looked up from tugging here and there at her dress, fussing with the velvet's nap. "Who's the other witness?" she asked.

Sam smiled. "You'll see."

* * *

When the elevator doors opened, Sam raced out first to look up and down the corridor. Laura thought he was acting very strangely indeed. More keyed up than she'd ever seen him. Nervous, actually. Like a long-tailed cat in a roomful of rockers, as Nana used to say.

Well, she wasn't all that calm herself. And, sad to say, she wasn't all that excited. A bride ought to be full of happy anticipation on her wedding day, not full of doubts and suspicions.

Sam was in the corridor now, pointing this way and that, like a traffic cop.

"I'm going to check to make sure Judge Randle is in his chambers. Charlie, how about waiting down there by the water fountain?"

"Sure thing, boss."

"I'll wait there, too," Laura said, following in Charlie's tracks. "I could use a drink of water."

Sam snagged her arm. "That's bad luck," he said. "Brides aren't supposed to use drinking fountains on their wedding days."

"That's ridiculous."

"Hey. I don't make up these rules." He propelled her along the corridor to a door marked 'Private,' then told her, "This is the bride's waiting room. Go on in, and I'll come get you when the judge is ready for us."

Laura balked. "Isn't there some rule about brides not having to wait alone? Can't you stay with me, Sam? Please?"

"I'll be back in a couple of minutes."

He seemed almost too eager to get away. "You're

not having second thoughts about this, are you? About the wedding? Because if you are..."

He cut off her words with a kiss. One of those all-out, tongue-touching, breath-robbing, spine-melting kisses that he was so good at. Then he turned the knob on the door and gave her a little shove inside the room.

A gray-haired man in a dark blue suit was standing by the window, gazing out. At the sight of him, Laura whispered frantically over her shoulder to Sam, "I don't want to wait in here and feel like a fool in front of a complete stranger."

But Sam was already closing the door on her. The latch sounded a definitive click at her back just as the gray-haired man turned from the window to face her, and for a second Laura felt as if she were looking in a mirror.

"Daddy?" The word left her lips in soft, almost childlike whisper.

"Laura!" He started across the room, arms stretched out to her, tears glistening in his blue eyes. "Look at you! Just look at you! My little girl's all grown up!"

It was a good thing he hugged her so tightly, otherwise Laura would have crumpled to the floor. Then he led her to a chair, saying "I think we both need to sit down, sweetheart."

When he took her hands in his, all she could do was stare at the long fingers—just like hers—and the shape of his nails, identical to her own.

"We don't have much time, honey. I have to be back in Chicago in a couple hours. But Sam told me how much damage the divorce did to you, and I need to make this right."

"You left us." Her voice sounded small, as if she were six years old again.

"No. That's the thing, honey. I didn't." He squeezed her hands. "Your mother wanted the divorce. She wanted me out of her life. And your life, too."

"So you just left."

"Her! I left her, but I never left you. I came by the house every week, but she always sent you out someplace. I sent checks she never cashed. I sent birthday cards."

Laura thought of her shoebox filled with all the cards she'd ever received. None of them was from Oliver McNeal. "I never got them."

"I know. Every damned one came back marked Return to Sender." He twisted his wrist a fraction to consult his watch. "Ah, God, sweetheart. There's not enough time to tell you all the whys and the whens. But finally, I guess when you were about twelve, your mother told me you never wanted to see me again, that you'd said you wished I was dead."

"I never..."

He touched her cheek. "I know that now. But back then, sixteen years ago, I believed it. That's when I moved away and tried, for the sake of my own sanity, to make myself forget."

"Oh, Daddy." Tears started cascading from her eyes, plopping on the lap of her dress. "I'm so sorry. I'm so, so sorry."

"It wasn't your fault, Laura. Or mine." He sighed roughly. "But, look. That's all behind us now, right? This is your big day. You're getting married. And the baby!"

"Sam told you?"

"Yes, he told me, and it's the best news I've ever gotten in my life. I never remarried, so I don't have any other kids or any family at all. Now I've not only got my daughter back, but I'm going to be a grandfather. That's such wonderful news."

Laura nodded. Suddenly it was wonderful news. Suddenly everything was wonderful. There weren't any words to describe how her heart was feeling. She was about to babble something when Sam opened the door and stepped inside.

Zachary, S. U. was looking Seriously Unsure of himself just then. Sweating Undeniably.

"The judge is ready for us," Sam said, offering her his hand.

Laura's heart felt so full she could hardly breathe. So full and happy and complete. Sure. Utterly.

Charlie, with a grin permanently plastered on his lips, joined them in the judge's chambers, and while Sam had a last minute talk with Judge Randle, Laura whispered to her father.

"I don't usually dress this way, Daddy."

Oliver McNeal gave her an appreciative wink. "That's too bad, honey. You look good in blue."

"No, I mean..."

"Shh," he said. "I know what you mean. Sam told me about the day you came into his office. A lucky day for you both, I'd say."

It wasn't easy being grateful to Artie Hammerman for socking her in the eye, Laura thought, but that moment she was enormously grateful.

The judge crossed the room to introduce himself and to shake hands all around. When he took Laura's hand, the man said, "Ordinarily I don't perform the traditional wedding service, Miss McNeal, with the traditional vows. But Sam has asked me to make an exception this afternoon. I'm assuming that's all right with you?''

"Yes. Of course."

The judge straightened his black robe while the bride and groom and the witnesses took their places in front of him.

Laura stood with her arm linked through Sam's, savoring the lovely words of the ceremony—the dearly beloved and the for richer, for poorer and the in sickness and in health—even as she wondered why her almost-husband seemed to be finding the beautiful, age-old vows so amusing.

It didn't take too long, though, to discover why he couldn't wipe the silly grin off his face.

When the judge finally got to the end of Sam's vows, where he somberly intoned, ''...till death do you part?'' Sam didn't answer with the expected *I do*.

Instead, he just kept grinning as he bent his head and whispered, ''I told you so.''

* * * * *

presents the gripping miniseries

***WHERE TIME IS
OF THE ESSENCE
IN THE SEARCH
FOR TRUE LOVE....***

CINDERELLA FOR A NIGHT—on sale Sept. 2000
by **Susan Mallery** (IM #1029)

A THANKSGIVING TO REMEMBER—on sale Oct. 2000
by **Margaret Watson** (IM #1035)

A VERY...PREGNANT NEW YEAR'S—on sale Dec. 2000
by **Doreen Roberts** (IM #1047)

MY SECRET VALENTINE—on sale Jan. 2001
by **Marilyn Pappano** (IM #1053)

Don't miss an original
Silhouette Christmas anthology
**36 HOURS: THE CHRISTMAS
THAT CHANGED EVERYTHING**
with stories by
Mary Lynn Baxter, Marilyn Pappano, Christine Flynn
On sale November 2000

Available at yor favorite retail outlet.

Where love comes alive™

Visit Silhouette at www.eHarlequin.com   SIM36H

INTIMATE MOMENTS®
Silhouette®

presents a riveting 12-book continuity series:

A Year of loving dangerously

Where passion rules and nothing is what it seems...

When dishonor threatens a top-secret agency, the brave
men and women of SPEAR are prepared to risk it all as they
put their lives—and their hearts—on the line.

Available October 2000:

HER SECRET WEAPON

by Beverly Barton

The only way agent Burke Lonigan can protect his pretty
assistant is to offer her the safety of his privileged lifestyle—as
his wife. But what will Burke do when he discovers Callie is
the same beguiling beauty he shared one forgotten night of
passion with—and the mother of his secret child?

*Available only from Silhouette Intimate Moments
at your favorite retail outlet.*

Silhouette®

Where love comes alive™

Visit Silhouette at www.eHarlequin.com

SIMAYOLD5

If you enjoyed what you just read,
then we've got an offer you can't resist!

Take 2 bestselling love stories FREE!

Plus get a FREE surprise gift!

Clip this page and mail it to Silhouette Reader Service™

IN U.S.A.	**IN CANADA**
3010 Walden Ave.	P.O. Box 609
P.O. Box 1867	Fort Erie, Ontario
Buffalo, N.Y. 14240-1867	L2A 5X3

YES! Please send me 2 free Silhouette Intimate Moments® novels and my free surprise gift. Then send me 6 brand-new novels every month, which I will receive months before they're available in stores. In the U.S.A., bill me at the bargain price of $3.80 plus 25¢ delivery per book and applicable sales tax, if any*. In Canada, bill me at the bargain price of $4.21 plus 25¢ delivery per book and applicable taxes**. That's the complete price and a savings of at least 10% off the cover prices—what a great deal! I understand that accepting the 2 free books and gift places me under no obligation ever to buy any books. I can always return a shipment and cancel at any time. Even if I never buy another book from Silhouette, the 2 free books and gift are mine to keep forever. So why not take us up on our invitation. You'll be glad you did!

245 SEN C226
345 SEN C227

Name _____ (PLEASE PRINT)

Address _____ Apt.# _____

City _____ State/Prov. _____ Zip/Postal Code _____

* Terms and prices subject to change without notice. Sales tax applicable in N.Y.
** Canadian residents will be charged applicable provincial taxes and GST.
All orders subject to approval. Offer limited to one per household.
® are registered trademarks of Harlequin Enterprises Limited.

INMOM00 ©1998 Harlequin Enterprises Limited

Silhouette invites you to come
back to Whitehorn, Montana...

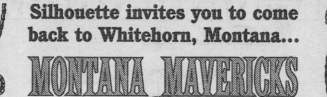

MONTANA MAVERICKS

WED IN WHITEHORN—
12 BRAND-NEW stories that capture living
and loving beneath the Big Sky where legends
live on and love lasts forever!

MM

June 2000—
Lisa Jackson *Lone Stallion's Lady* (#1)

July 2000—
Laurie Paige *Cheyenne Bride* (#2)

August 2000—
Jennifer Greene *You Belong to Me* (#3)

September 2000—
Victoria Pade *The Marriage Bargain* (#4)

And the adventure continues...

Available at your favorite retail outlet.

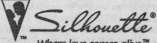

Silhouette®
Where love comes alive™

INTIMATE MOMENTS®

™ Silhouette®

COMING NEXT MONTH

CMN0900